A LOVE SO DEADLY

TO THE BONE BOOK TWO

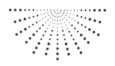

LILI VALENTE

A LOVE SO DEADLY

To The Bone
Book Two

By Lili Valente

ABOUT THE BOOK

GABE: Caitlin is everything I never knew I needed. But I'm not just bad for her—I'm toxic.

If I stay, I'll destroy her, but I can't keep my hands to myself. I keep reaching for the only good thing left in the world, but I don't know how much longer I can hold on.

Especially when a monster lurks in the darkness, waiting for me to drop my guard so he can take what's mine.

Take her, lock her up, and play those ugly games I know he's played before.

What once was dangerous is turning deadly, and only the devil knows if either Caitlin or I

will make it out alive.

Alert: A Love So Deadly is a full-length novel and book two in a continuing story. It should be read after A Love So Dangerous.

"And softness came from the starlight
and filled me full to the bone."

— W.B. YEATS

CHAPTER ONE

GABE

The course of true love never did run smooth. -
Shakespeare

can't sleep.

      I lie in bed for hours, but I can't sleep and I can't quit thinking about her.

It's all I've done all day. I keep seeing her face in that moment before I bolted, with her cheeks flushed and wet with tears, and the shattered look in her eyes. I keep hearing the way her voice cracked when she told me she loved me, feeling the hairline fractures in my heart getting wider and wider.

She loves me; I love her.

She needs me; I need her.

All the other truths keep swirling around in my head, insisting they're relevant, but in the end it comes back to loving and needing and wondering why doing the right thing feels so wrong. I tell myself that this hurt now will spare her bigger hurt later, but as I lie in the darkness, watching my ceiling fan spin in circles, a voice deep inside insists I haven't given Caitlin the credit she deserves.

Life has knocked her down again and again, but she keeps getting back up. Her dad is a waste, but Caitlin never let that be an excuse to give up on making her life better. Her mom abandoned the family when Caitlin was twelve, and Caitlin stepped up and helped her older sister take care of the younger kids. Her sister left when Caitlin was seventeen, and Caitlin stood strong and stubbornly refused to let her family fall apart.

A month ago, I would have said she sacrificed herself for the kids, but now I know that's not accurate. Caitlin is a good person, but she doesn't do anything she doesn't want to do. She did what she did because, at the end of the day, the people she loves mean more to her than anything else in the world. Those kids are her biggest source of pride, their happiness the soul food that keeps her going. Her love isn't a stone tied around her neck; it's the source of her impressive strength.

She is tougher than anyone in her life gives her credit for—even me.

Chances are she's tough enough to hear my truth, and to walk the last steps along the road with me. In my heart, I know she'd want to do it. She'd want to know that I wasn't alone, that the most important person in my life was with me. And she has to know that person is her, that she is...everything.

I was certain she did, but that was before I took a chainsaw to her heart earlier today.

I squeeze my eyes closed and curse beneath my breath.

Have I fucked things up again? Have I made everything worse, when all I was trying to do was make the kindest choice possible?

I wish I had parents like the ones on the television shows I loved as a kid. I wish I had someone I could trust to give me good advice. But Aaron and Deborah have never been my kind of people. We might as well be from two different planets, as was evidenced when I got back from Caitlin's house late this afternoon and confessed to my parents that my symptoms were getting worse.

My mom spent approximately two minutes sniffling before heading into her office to arrange for plane flights and reservations for the hospice I picked out when I decided not to go through with the surgery. I sat in silence with my dad, listening to my mother's voice drift into the sitting room until I heard her place a call to her interior decorator, to discuss having my room packed up and remodeled.

Not quite ready to contemplate every trace of my existence being wiped away, I left. My father, who I know will never forgive me for "giving up," didn't even say goodbye.

I know they love me. I know they aren't as cold as they appear—this is just how they deal with their feelings of powerlessness and grief—but I don't want my mother's or father's eyes to be the last thing I see. I want to be looking into Caitlin's green eyes, the only eyes that have ever seen every secret part of me, the eyes of the only person who has ever made me feel normal, whole, and completely loved.

I turn things over and over and still can't decide what the right answer is, but I know I can't stay in bed a second longer. I shove off the sheets and swing my legs down to the floor, ignoring the faint aching in my skull. The pain has remained under control since I took a pill after getting back from Caitlin's, and I haven't had another dizzy spell since right after dinner. I should be okay to drive, and even if I weren't, I'd still go. I suddenly need to get out of the house. I have to *go* somewhere, even if I'm not sure where I'm headed.

Or so I tell myself.

I tell myself I'm just going for a drive, but I'm not surprised when I find myself steering the Beamer toward Caitlin's. It's after midnight and I doubt she's awake—and I'm not ready to go back on my decision to end it—but looking at the darkened house and knowing she's inside will be more comforting than any other view in Giffney.

I turn off the headlights before I pull onto her street, not wanting her to see them sweep across the curtains if she's still awake. I let the car idle almost noiselessly halfway around the cul-de-sac before I roll down my window, shove the car into park, and cut the engine.

Seconds later, the car parked in front of me— a dark sedan with a dent on one side of the roof —roars to life. The driver swerves away from the curb, tires squealing as he pulls away and guns it toward the stop sign at the end of the road. I flick on my lights, figuring the psycho must be smashed, and I should get his plate in case he hits someone, when I see a piece of threadbare fabric peeking out of the sedan's trunk.

The fabric is bright pink, a garish color that's horribly familiar.

It's the same color as the fat cat tee shirt Caitlin loves to wear to bed. The shirt is three sizes too big, and so thin from washing that it's transparent. Normally I would approve, but the obese cat sprawled across the front of the shirt, scratching his balls, negates any sex appeal.

I see the flash of fabric, and immediately, in my mind, Caitlin is in that trunk. Caitlin is being kidnapped by a man in a dark blue sedan driving like a maniac.

A man I might lose if I don't follow him. Right. Fucking. Now.

I twist the key and slam the Beamer into drive, shooting off after the sedan, catching sight of him as he pulls right onto Newberry, headed away from downtown. I stop at the stop sign, cursing the white minivan that shoots past, coming between me and the sedan. As soon as the van is clear, I turn, fingers squeezing the steering wheel as my heart pounds and my mouth goes dry with fear. I weave over the center line, keeping the car, and that scrap of pink fabric, in my sight.

A voice in my head says I'm being crazy, but I can't shake the feeling that Caitlin's in trouble. I can't see much more than an outline of the driver's head, but it's obviously a man driving the car. And why the fuck would a man have pink fabric, the exact horrible shade as Caitlin's tee shirt, in his trunk?

He's got a daughter who plays soccer, and she left

her jersey in the trunk. He's got a wife who boxed up a load of clothes to take to the Salvation Army and he hasn't gotten around to dropping them off yet.

There are lots of reasons. But none of them explain why this strange car was parked outside of Caitlin's house in the middle of the night, and is driving like a bat out of hell.

I back off the minivan's ass, easing off the pedal until I'm a respectable two car lengths away, and slip in my Bluetooth earpiece. I voice dial Caitlin's landline, but keep my eyes on the sedan. The driver has slowed and is keeping the car between the lines, but he's still going at least ten miles over the limit.

Why is he in such a hurry? There is hardly anyone on the road this time of night, and Giffney isn't that big. He's going to get where he's going soon enough sticking to forty miles per hour.

The phone rings and rings, until finally I'm sent to the answering machine.

"This is Gabe," I say. "Caitlin, I need you to call me back. Right away."

I end the call and redial immediately. The phone rings, and the answering machine picks up, but just as I'm leaving another message for Caitlin, Danny picks up the phone.

"What the fuck," he says, his voice slurred with sleep. "It's the middle of the fucking night, asshole. Haven't you made my sister cry enough for one day?"

Something inside me cringes thinking about Caitlin crying, but there's no time to apologize. "Danny, listen to me. I need you to go upstairs and get your sister."

"Fuck you," he says.

"Danny, please," I insist, panic that he might hang up straining my voice. "Please, just...go make sure she's up there. You don't have to wake her. Just make sure she's safe, and come back and let me know."

Danny mumbles something I can't understand, but I'm assuming is more profanity.

"Please, Danny," I beg, fist tightening around the wheel as I make a sharp left turn onto county road 50, following the sedan as he takes the back roads out of town. "I'm worried about her. I'll drop a hundred dollar bill in the mailbox for you tomorrow, if you'll just let me know she's upstairs sleeping."

"Keep your money," he snaps.

There's a sharp clacking sound, loud enough to make me wince, but the line doesn't go dead. I strain to hear what's going on and imagine I can make out Danny's footsteps thudding up the stairs. A minute passes—a minute that I know is a minute, not an eternity, because I can see the clock on my console holding steady at 12:21—

and then I definitely hear footsteps on the stairs.

The steps are faster, louder, giving me a clue that Caitlin isn't safe in her bed, even before a breathless Danny picks up the phone.

"She's not there," he pants, not sounding so tough anymore. He sounds as scared as I feel, and so young I feel like shit for not being able to protect him from whatever has happened. "She's not in bed and the lamp near the window is knocked over. The bulb is shattered all over the floor."

I curse, fingers tightening on the wheel, barely resisting the urge to slam the gas pedal closer to the floor and shorten the distance between me and the sedan. But if this guy has Caitlin, he's going to be on the lookout for someone following him. I don't want to get into a high speed chase with the girl I love knocking around in the trunk. She could already be hurt. I need to keep my thoughts clear, and my head on straight, and do whatever it takes to make sure I get her back in one piece.

And make sure I have the chance to tear the man who took her into strips of bleeding, aching, dying flesh for daring to touch her. I'll kill him if he's hurt her.

I may kill him anyway.

"I'm going to call 911," Danny says, pulling my

thoughts back to the boy on the other end of the line.

"No, wait," I say, though a part of me insists it's a good idea.

But I don't know who has Caitlin, or what he might know about our extracurricular activities. There's a chance that her kidnapping is unrelated to the things we've been doing, but I can't know that for sure, and until I do, I can't put her future at risk. I don't want the cops called in until I'm sure I can't handle this myself.

"Wait until I get a better idea of where this guy is going," I say. "I'm following the man who took her."

"What?" Danny says. "How?"

"I pulled up outside your house as the man was pulling away. I saw part of Caitlin's pink tee shirt sticking out of the trunk."

Danny curses. "What are you going to do? You have to get her back, Gabe."

"I'm going to get her back," I promise. "Hang tight by the phone. If I need you to call the police, I'll call. If you don't hear from me in twenty minutes, get one of the cell phones from Caitlin's bedside table. Call 911 from the cell, and leave an anonymous tip that you saw a blue sedan headed east on route 50. Tell them you heard a girl screaming inside the trunk. Don't tell them who you are."

"Can you hear her screaming?" Danny asks, his voice shaking.

"No, I can't," I say softly. "I'm going to drive now, Danny. Hang in there, don't tell any of the other kids, and don't give your name to the police. I'm going to bring Caitlin home, or die trying."

"Okay," Danny says. A moment later the line goes dead, seconds before the sedan takes a sharp turn to the left, headed down a gravel road.

I fight the urge to brake, keeping the Beamer headed straight on 50 even though my heart surges up into my throat as I watch the car with Caitlin in it rush away to the north. That last turn was too sudden, even for a crap driver like this guy. He must suspect I'm following him. I have to keep going until the next bend, then turn around and retrace my route with the headlights off and put him off his guard. I should be able to figure out where he went. It hasn't rained in weeks. The gravel is dry and will hang in the air after being disturbed. All I'll have to do is hang back and follow the trail.

Around the next turn, I veer onto the shoulder and spin in a tight circle, flipping my lights off as I start back the way I came. It's dark as the bottom level of hell out here in the country, away from the lights of town and the street-lights of the suburbs. But there's a half moon in the sky, giving off enough light that I'm able to keep the car on the right side of the road. I spot the turn onto the gravel road—Ellery Avenue—and turn right.

My heart is still beating so fast and hard it feels like someone is punching me in the throat with every throb of my pulse, but the knowledge that I'm back on the fucker's trail is comforting. So is the haze of dust hanging in the air above the road. I'm starting to think this is going to work, and I'll be able to tail the guy to wherever he's taking Caitlin without being observed, when a lightning bolt of pain zigzags through my skull.

It starts in my neck and rips through the center of my head to explode behind my right eye. I see dying stars—flashes of orange and deep red that morph into patches of blinding white light—and the world does a three sixty.

I cry out and slam on the brakes.

Or, I think I do. I tell my foot to push down, but I'm not sure if it obeys. I'm not sure where I am, who I am. All I know is that I'm blind and the world is spinning. Up is down, right is left, I can't see and I can't nail down my position in space. And then, like a light switched off, everything goes black, and I am alone with the pain that roars inside me like a monster hungry for blood.

CHAPTER TWO

CAITLIN

It is not a secret if it is known by three people. –Irish proverb

*D*ust. Old Clothes. Mold.

Something bitter and metallic, with an overtone of rot.

The smells are the first thing I'm aware of. They are awful smells, smells that remind me of somewhere I've been before. I can't remember the place, but I know it's nowhere I want to be again. I *know*, even before my eyes creak open to see the dusty floor of Pitt's attic forming my horizon line, and a single, bare, orange bulb dangling from the ceiling like a sickly little sun.

I blink, my lashes catching on the mattress beneath my cheek.

The mattress. I'm lying on the mattress Pitt's mother slept on, wept on, *died* on.

My entire body convulses. I roll onto the floor with a spasm of arms and legs and a frantic clutching of my stomach. I roll and keep rolling until something catches hard around my ankle, bruising the bone, and I can't roll any further. I sit up, sobs catching in my throat as I reach for my leg. The world blurs as I move and a dull, throbbing pain starts at my left temple, near the place where Pitt must have hit me to knock me out.

Knocked me out and brought me back to his attic, where God only knows what he plans to do to me. And there will be no one to stop him, no one riding to the rescue. No one will *ever* think to look for me here except Gabe, and Gabe is gone.

I have to get out; I have to fucking get out.

I find the source of the pain around my ankle. A handcuff circles my leg just above my ankle-bone. The other half of the cuff is attached to a length of heavy chain tied around one of the support beams not far from the mattress. I pick up the chain and track my way down it with trembling fingers, but every link is strong and there's no way I'm going to be able to knock over the thick, wooden support beam without a sledgehammer.

I'm caught. Trapped. There's no way out.

The truth is still settling in—hands wrapping around my throat, promising to choke the life out of me—when the trap door on the far right of the attic opens and the collapsible stairs descend. A shaft of brighter light pierces the orange gloom, casting a jagged, sharp-edged square of white on the wall.

I back away, arms trembling at my sides, getting as close to the window as I can. But I'm still two feet from the sill, far enough that no one looking in would see me, and I know this house is so deep in the middle of nowhere there will be no one to hear me scream.

Still, I have to grip my throat with one hand to hold back a panicked whimper as Pitt appears at the top of the stairs and steps into the attic. He's wearing all black—black jeans, black tee shirt, and a black sock cap that covers his thinning blond hair—and I'm possessed by the nasty feeling that the tables have been turned, and I don't like it.

Not one little bit.

"You're awake," he says, his tiny, pink-rimmed blue eyes looking even smaller with the bulb overhead casting dark shadows above his cheekbones. "I was worried. You barely moved the entire time I was carrying you."

I don't say a word. I watch him, fighting to keep the fear and panic from my face, resisting the urge to pull my pink sleep shirt lower around my thighs. I don't want to give him the satisfaction of knowing how terrified I am. Terrified—for myself, and for the kids, who are going to wake up tomorrow morning and be scared out of their minds when they realize I'm gone.

"I'm not going to hurt you," Pitt says, in that same smug, condescending voice he used when he talked about Danny's behavior problems and lack of potential at all those stupid conferences.

I can't believe I sat across from him and talked about my brother like I was talking to a halfway reasonable person. I always knew Pitt was a jerk and a bully and probably had a penis the size of a shriveled gherkin—no man with even an average-sized dick would be so petty—but I'd never dreamt he was capable of breaking into someone's house and kidnapping them. Even when I learned what he'd done to his mom, I hadn't imagined he'd do the same thing to anyone else. I had assumed it was a twisted, mother-son thing that had played out its sad, miserable course, and been put to rest.

Obviously, I was wrong, and I'm not near as

smart as I think I am. If I were, Pitt would never have traced that blackmail note back to me.

That has to be it. That has to be why I'm here. Somehow, he must have figured out that I wrote the note, no matter how careful I was to type the entire thing and print it out at the copy shop in town instead of using the printer at home.

But how? How the hell did he—

"Did you hear me?" Pitt breaks into my thoughts, making me flinch as he takes a sudden step closer.

I try to take a mirror step back, forgetting I'm tethered, and nearly fall.

"Careful." Pitt chuckles. "You're all arms and legs aren't you? Like a little filly."

"You have to let me go," I say, liking the affectionate note in his voice even less than the smug one. If Pitt thinks I'm going to play house with him, or touch him, or do anything else with him, he's very fucking mistaken.

I'll chew my own leg off first.

Pitt shakes his head, pulling his cap from his head as he turns to pace across the attic, closer to where I found the DVDs. The area that was once filled with boxes is now barren, proving Pitt has learned not to keep his goodies where someone sneaking in the window can find them.

Not that he has any goodies left anymore.

"No, Caitlin. I can't let you go." His voice is

muffled now that his back is turned, but I can still hear him loud and clear. "You took something that belongs to me, and now you're going to help get it back."

"How did you find out?" There's no point in pretending I wasn't the one who stole from him. He obviously knows. Now I want to know how. I want to know how Gabe and I screwed up, so we don't do it again.

Gabe is done with you, and you're never leaving this room. Your days of breaking and entering and living to plan the next job are over.

I clench my jaw, refusing to listen to the ominous voice in my head.

"The dust." Pitt points to the floorboards. "I was able to get two clear footprints, but they were so small..."

He laughs as he turns back to me. "I thought it was a kid, one of my students. I was looking for your brother tonight, but then I saw those little black combat boots in your closet and the tread matched up just right..." He shakes his head. "I was surprised, Caitlin. I really was. You do such a good job of hiding what you are, coming off so sweet and honest and concerned about your brother." He tips his chin down, casting his eyes in deeper shadow before he adds in an uglier voice, "but you're just lying, thieving trash. Like the rest of your family."

"At least I'm not a murderer," I say, voice shaking.

Pitt smiles, a horrible smile that makes my belly churn as a tornado of acid sweeps across my stomach lining. "I spent over a month breaking in to little boys' rooms because of you, Caitlin, and that really isn't my thing. But I couldn't let it go. You had to have known I would never let it go, not until I had them back with me. Where they belong."

"You're not getting the DVDs back," I say. "Not from me. I don't know where they are. My partner hid them."

"A partner?" Pitt cocks his head, but I can't tell if he's really surprised.

"Yeah, my partner," I say. "He handles that kind of thing, and he's going to be very fucking upset when he finds out I'm missing. It won't take him long to figure out where I am. You should let me go."

"No," Pitt says, but I hear a hint of doubt in his voice.

"Just let me go," I insist. "I won't tell anyone what happened. Not even my partner. I'll just go home and—"

"You're not going anywhere until I get what's mine!"

I cringe away from the fury in his voice, arms flinching up to cover my head before I can stop myself. I drop my hands back to my sides as quickly as I can, but I'm shaking all over and I know Pitt's seen it, seen how scared I am.

He sees it, and he likes it. I swear it's like he grows three inches as he stands up straighter, spine stretching as he feeds on my fear.

"If that's true, then you're right. Your partner will be able to figure out where you are...sooner or later," Pitt says. "And when he does, I'll be ready for him, and make sure he knows how very upset I am, and what it's going to take to get you back."

A cold ball of fear knots in my chest, but I do my best to keep my expression neutral. Pitt can't know the truth. If he figures out no one is coming for me, I'll have no leverage at all.

"He's no dummy," I say. "He's not going to walk up to your front door and ring the bell. We broke into your house once without you knowing about it. He'll be able to do it again. You have to sleep sometime..."

I let my words trail off as I lift one shoulder. The unspoken threat hangs heavy in the air for a moment before Pitt grunts.

"Then I'll take the offensive." He crosses to the left side of the room, reaching up to adjust something in the shadows near the rafters. I can't see what it is, but his next words give me a pretty good idea.

"You can give me your partner's name and address, and I'll send him a free preview," he says, still tinkering in the shadows. "Everything's ready to go. I installed the camera and the new recording system a few weeks ago so I'd be prepared...just in case."

"In case of what?" My throat threatens to close as a red light flashes on above Pitt's head and I realize I'm being recorded.

"Well," Pitt says, voice pitched differently, lower and more confident, as if he's aware of being on camera, too. "As soon as I realized the DVDs were missing, I knew that there was a chance they had been destroyed, or hidden somewhere I'd never be able to find them. I knew there was a chance they were gone forever, and I would need to find...a replacement."

I swallow, pulse fluttering wildly at my throat as Pitt walks toward me.

"Well, not a replacement. No one can replace Mother," he says, voice soft, chilling. "Nothing can ever take the place of the memories you stole from me, but new memories can be made."

Not new memories, new trophies.

Gabe and I may, or may not, be sociopaths, but Pitt is a flat out psychopath, a monster with a taste for human suffering who looks like he's on his way to being a serial killer.

If I don't find a way to escape, Pitt will kill

me...eventually, of that there is no doubt in my mind. It will simply be a matter of how many days, or months, or years he'll keep me captive, torturing me the way he did his mother, before he gets bored and decides it's time to slip a lethal overdose into my food.

The thought sends a wave of terror and rage sweeping through me so powerful my trembling becomes quaking. I grit my teeth and clench my hands into fists, but no matter how hard I try, I can't quit shaking like it's nine degrees in the attic instead of ninety.

"Take off your shirt, Caitlin," Pitt says, a gleam in his eye that is more predatory than sexual. But it doesn't matter, because I'm not wearing anything but black bikini panties under my sleep shirt and I refuse to be all-but-naked in front of this man.

"No," I say, in a low, firm voice that sounds like I'm talking to a dog. I might as well be. Pitt's worse than a dog, he's an abomination, a freak of nature that should have been put down before he could grow fangs.

"Take it off," he repeats. "We earn our privileges here, and clothes are a privilege, not a necessity. Not in heat like this."

"No." I edge toward the mattress, eyes darting back and forth, scanning the floor, looking for something to use as a weapon.

"You'll be more comfortable," Pitt says in an upbeat voice. "And I bet your partner will enjoy seeing you naked. You're fucking him, aren't you?"

I press my lips together, fighting a whimper as Pitt gets closer, so close he'll be touching me soon if I don't do something. *Find* something.

My panicked gaze lands on the box of stuffed animals, but there's nothing in the soggy cardboard filled with moldy toys that will do any damage. Pitt is only five six and on the slim side, but he was strong enough to carry me out of my house and up the stairs to the attic. I have to find something heavy or sharp or—

The tea set.

The porcelain tea set that made me want to cry last time I was in this attic is still there on the ground, laid out for a party. The cups and saucers are too small to do any damage, but the pot is grapefruit-sized, maybe big enough to knock Pitt out if I use enough force, and take him by surprise.

I turn back to Pitt and reach for the bottom of my shirt. "Okay." I edge along the end of the mattress, toward the tea set on the far side. "I'll take it off, but I don't want you to look. Turn your back."

Pitt stops, crossing his arms. "Why would I do that?"

"Because you're not interested in seeing me naked," I say, praying I'm right. "I can tell it isn't like that for you."

Pitt smiles, sending my heart diving into my stomach. "Oh, it *is* like that, Caitlin. It very much *is*, but you're right, I'm not going to touch you." He steps closer, showing no sign of stopping or turning his back.

I shuffle another step closer to the tea set, holding Pitt's gaze as I keep the teapot in my peripheral vision, forcing myself to wait to reach for it, knowing I'll only have one chance.

"But later, when I go back and watch the tape," Pitt continues, his voice sludgy and slick, like slime oozing between my toes. "I'm going to get hard, and I'm going to take out my cock, and I'm going to jerk myself until I come all over the screen, all over your pretty face. I'll do it again and again, as many times as I want, because you are mine now. And when I'm tired of this tape, we'll make another, and another, until I have a new collection to fill the void left behind by what you stole from me."

I bite my lip, holding back a scream. I hold my terror in, allowing the tension and fear and panic to build inside, fueling my body, tightening my muscles, giving me strength.

One shot, one shot, and I'm not going to

screw it up, I'm not going to let Pitt's prophecy come true, I'm not going to be his victim.

"Now, take off your shirt." Pitt steps closer, until I could brush his chest with my fingertips if I held out my arm. "Show me your tits."

I swallow, blood rushing in my ears, and then, with one swift movement, I rip my shirt over my head and throw it at his face. His hands come up a second too late to catch it and while he fumbles with the fabric, I whirl, snatching up the teapot and bringing it over my head.

I don't think about the fact that I'm basically naked, or that I'm inches shorter and smaller than Pitt, or that I'm shackled and he's free. I come at him with all my rage and hatred and loathing, I come at him like *I* am the monster and he's the bug I'm going to squash beneath my foot.

I bring the pot down with every bit of strength in my body, a savage sound erupting from my lips as it shatters on his skull. The skin on his forehead bursts and blood rushes from the wound, but I don't take time to appreciate the crimson running into his eyes. I'm already lifting my hands back into the air, threading my palms together into a single combined fist and bringing it back down on top of his head. I land two more blows—pounding his skull like I'm driving a fence post into the ground with my bare hands—

before he lunges forward, tackling me, sending us both flying.

My back hits the mattress and my breath rushes out. Before I can pull in another, Pitt's hands are around my throat.

He screams, howling into my face, blood dripping from the wound on his forehead to fall onto my cheeks, my lips, into my mouth as I gasp for air. I taste the salty filth of him and know I would be sick if I could pull in a breath. I bring my hands to his face, shoving at his nose and mouth, gouging at his eyes, but it's like he can't feel my fingers stabbing away at him. His grip only tightens, and soon the air around his face goes blurry and gray, then fuzzy and black, and then there are flashes of light bursting in front of my eyes and my hands begin to go numb.

I flail my arms, but I'm not sure if I'm hitting him anymore. I'm not sure of anything except that I am dying, and Pitt is getting it all on tape.

My head is pounding, but my heart is slowing. The frantic thrum in my chest stutters, skipping a beat, then two. I lose sensation in my limbs and my vision narrows to a pinprick of light at the center of a long tunnel of black. I'm seconds away from passing out—passing out and sleeping my way through the last few seconds of my life— when something hits Pitt, knocking him off my prone body, and air rushes into my lungs.

CHAPTER THREE

CAITLIN

*May the devil make a ladder of your backbone
and pluck apples in the garden of hell.* —Irish curse

My back arches and pain shoots through my nerve-endings as I suck in one greedy breath after another, agony slamming from my fingers to my toes, before rocketing back to my head, making me groan. My head feels like it's going to explode. My eye sockets ache and my temples throb like someone took a hammer to my skull and my throat hurts so badly I can't believe I can still draw in breath.

But I can. I'm not dead. I'm alive. I'm alive and breathing, and slowly, the shadowed ceiling of the attic comes back into focus.

The moment the agony becomes manageable, I sit up, shoving myself into a seated position with half-numb hands, and falling onto my hands and knees on the mattress.

"Gabe." I croak his name, tears springing to my eyes as my breath shudders in and out and relief floods through my chest.

I don't know how he knew, how he found me, but there he is, the man I love, pinning Pitt to the ground, wrapping his hands around the monster's throat, showing Pitt what it feels like to be on the receiving end of a strangling. It's bizarre to see Gabe not dressed in his blacks in a situation like this. His light blue polo and dark blue jeans seem too civilized for the setting, making the moment even more surreal.

So surreal that Pitt is turning purple by the time I realize Gabe doesn't intend to stop.

He's going to kill him. Gabe is going to kill Pitt. I know I should stop him, and we should go to the police, but a part of me doesn't want to. A part of me is crouched on her haunches like an animal, howling for Gabe to finish this. She can't wait to see Pitt dead, to dance around his body and celebrate the stilling of his evil, fucking heart.

I would have let it happen, I know I would have, but just as Pitt is going still, Gabe cries out, hands flying to grip his head. He moans and sways, falling off of Pitt, hitting the floorboards with a thud that makes me flinch.

I'm already on my way to him when Pitt sucks in a liquid breath and begins to choke.

I freeze, gaze flicking from Gabe moaning on the floor, to Pitt choking right beside him. I have a split second to make my choice, and then I'm on top of Pitt, picking up where Gabe left off.

I don't know what's happening to Gabe, but if Pitt gets up off the ground, we're both screwed. I'm still chained to the wall. If Pitt recovers enough to get up and out of reach, I will have lost the upper hand and might never get another chance to save myself, to save the man I love.

The man who calls my name as I straddle Pitt's chest and lock my hands around the bastard's throat, leaning forward until all of my body weight is bearing down on his windpipe, sealing it off. I hear the encouragement in Gabe's voice, know he wants me to do this, to save myself, to save us, and I grit my teeth and hold on.

Pitt thrashes beneath me, but not with near the strength he was thrashing when Gabe started this. He's weak and that one gasp of air he managed to suck in isn't going to hold him for long. He's going to die. I'm going to kill him. I can feel the truth in the way my fingers crack as they dig into his flesh, see it in the way Pitt's beady

LILI VALENTE

eyes bulge from his face, smell it in the tangy, sour smell of urine that soaks the front of Pitt's pants, making me grateful I'm sitting on his chest.

I don't want any more of his piss or blood or spit or breath on me. I want this to end. Now. And then I want to set everything on fire and watch it burn.

I grit my teeth, a sob catching in my chest as Pitt continues to wiggle beneath me for what feels like an eternity. His death stretches on forever and then...suddenly, it's quiet. It's quiet and still and I can feel the change in air pressure that is one less soul occupying this space, one less monster to hide in the shadows, looking for something beautiful to destroy.

I don't know if I'm a monster like him or something else, but I know that I'm so fucking glad it's over.

Slowly, with a concentrated effort, I unpeel my fingers from Pitt's throat, one by one, staying perched on his body long enough to make certain he's not coming back to life before I turn and half-fall to the ground beside Gabe. I'm crying, sobbing, tears streaming from my face, but not because of Pitt, at least not just because of that. It's because of all of it, because it's too much and I don't know how to hold everything that's happened in the past few minutes in my

34

head. I just know I need to get to Gabe, to make sure he's okay. If he's okay, everything will be okay.

"Gabe? Are you all right? What's wrong?" I reach out, barely able to touch his furrowed brow with my fingers. My chain is too short to let me cradle his head in my arms, but I pet his hair with a trembling hand, praying for him to open his eyes.

"Gabe, please," I rasp, emotion and the bruises on my throat making my voice thin. "I can't finish this without you. Please, open your eyes. Please, come back to me."

"I love you," he says, the words thick and slurred, but so beautiful they make me cry harder.

"I love you, too," I sob. "What's wrong? What's happening?"

"I'll be okay in a minute," he says, sounding steadier, though he doesn't open his eyes. "They're coming in waves. I have…time between. Sometimes hours."

"What's coming in waves?" I ask, a horrible knot of fear forming in my stomach.

"I have…" He sighs and finally his eyes open, his stunning eyes that are full of love and pain and relief. "I'm feeling better. He's dead?"

I nod, not trusting myself to say the words out loud. I'm holding together so far, but eventually the knowledge that I've killed a man is going to penetrate and I'm going to be devastated.

Or not, which would be devastating in its own way.

Gabe blinks, but doesn't seem surprised, or displeased. "Then we should start...taking care of things. We might not have much time."

I shake my head. "Tell me what's wrong. Are you sick? Is that why you couldn't run the other night? Is that why you're trying to leave me?"

"I can't leave you," Gabe says. "I didn't last a day. I missed you so much I drove by to sit out on the street and watch the house. I would have ended up in your bedroom, begging for forgiveness, if I hadn't seen Pitt's car pull away."

So that's how he found me. My shoulders sag. I'm relieved that I'm safe, relieved that I'm not crazy, and that Gabe does care about me as much as I care about him. The relief lasts only a few seconds, however, before Gabe says—

"I told Danny to call the police if he didn't hear back from me in twenty minutes. I blacked out on the way here and when I came to, my cell wasn't getting service. I was going to turn around and drive closer to town to call him, but then I saw the railroad trestle. I realized Pitt must have you, and had to get to you. I couldn't think of anything else."

He lifts a hand, cradling my head. "I'm so glad

I got here in time. I'm so glad you finished it. You did the right thing."

I take a shaky breath, love and fear and adrenaline mixing inside me until it feels like my heart is going to burst through my chest. "Why don't you go downstairs and call Danny, tell him not to call the police. I'll check Pitt's pockets to see if I can find a key to the cuffs."

Gabe pushes into a seated position, holding his head in a careful way that makes me think it must still be hurting. "No. They might get the phone records. It wouldn't look good for Pitt's last call to be made to your house."

"Okay, then we'll just have to hurry." I turn back to Pitt's body, clenching my teeth against the bile that rises in my throat as I force my hand into his urine-soaked pants pocket, searching for the key to the cuffs. I find it in his back pocket a moment later and glance back to tell Gabe, but he's already across the room at the attic stairs.

"I'm going to find bleach and something for you to wear. We'll have to burn your tee shirt along with the rest of it. It got blood on it while you were fighting Pitt."

I glance down, blinking in surprise. "I forgot I was naked."

"You're probably in shock," Gabe says. "Just get yourself free and wait here. I'll be right back."

"Look for a recording device while you're

down there," I say, already reaching down to unlock my bruised ankle. "Pitt was recording everything the past twenty minutes or so. I'm not sure what I said, but it was probably incriminating. We have to destroy it. And probably his hard drive while we're at it."

Gabe nods. "All right. Hang tight."

I unlock my ankle as Gabe thumps down the stairs and spring to my feet, making use of my newfound freedom to pad across the attic and rip the camera from its place in the rafters. I smash it to pieces on the floor, slamming it into the boards until it shatters to bits, shocked to discover how okay I am with being naked right now. I don't feel vulnerable the way I did when Pitt was ordering me to strip. I feel powerful, primal, ready to tear my enemy to pieces, bury the bones, and put this night behind me.

Maybe Gabe is right, and I am in shock, maybe not, I only know that when Gabe returns, and we start cleaning up the blood and mess, my hands get steadier. I don't tremble as I throw on a plain white tee shirt and a pair of men's khaki shorts, rolling the waistband over until the fabric is tight enough to stay on my hips. I move calmly from one task to another, and in ten minutes Gabe and I have everything in the house cleaned up, a suicide note emailed to the school from

Pitt's account, and Pitt's body positioned on the mattress.

"I'm going to soak the mattress and make it look like he dropped the lighter," Gabe says, pressing a soft kiss to my forehead before beginning to spray the kerosene we found in Pitt's garage over the body. "Run down to the garage and wipe down the inside of the trunk with the bleach cloth. Make sure you look for any stray blond hairs. If the fire department gets the fire contained before it reaches the garage, we don't want them to find any evidence that you were ever here."

"Meet me in two minutes, or I'm coming back up," I say, still worried about him, though he's been acting fine since he recovered.

"No, you head into the woods," Gabe says. "The police could be here any minute."

"That's why I'll be back up to check on you," I say, heading for the stairs, ignoring his protest that making sure I'm not caught is the top priority.

I don't want to lose my freedom, but I don't want to lose Gabe, either. He's necessary to my existence, even more so after tonight. He may have been part of the reason I was almost killed, but he also saved me. He's brought danger into my world, but he's also brought joy and passion and life.

I was only half alive before I met Gabe. I know that now. I was a shadow of my true self, going through the motions, spending my life responding instead of acting.

Now, I don't put out fires, I help light them, and I won't go back, not even for the kids. Maybe that makes me an awful person, as much as killing Pitt or stealing or anything else, but I can't help it. It's true. I won't give up Gabe, not for safety or love or family. He is a part of me, and I will never let him go.

By the time the police sirens pierce the still, humid air, the attic and the roof of Pitt's house are burning brightly enough to light up the night sky and Gabe and I are through the woods to the abandoned chat dump where he parked the Beamer.

I start around to the passenger's side, but he stops me with a hand on my arm and drops the keys into my hand.

"Just in case," he whispers. "I just got you back, I'm not going to risk an accident taking you away from me."

I nod, swallowing the questions on my lips until we're safe. I start the car and pull down the narrow gravel road, heading away from Pitt's house and the sirens growing closer and closer, howling like dogs chasing a train they're never going to catch. Gabe and I are gone, and all the evidence is burning away. Even if they get the fire put out, Pitt will be nothing but charred remains. There will be no fingerprints, no hair or spit or blood or anything to tie me and Gabe to Pitt's death.

Together, we've killed a man and gotten away with it and it feels…okay.

Not great, not a rush like the other jobs, when we could barely wait to get back to my house and make love, but okay. He was a horrible man who had already murdered one person, and who would have tortured and killed me if he'd had the chance. I can live with his blood on my hands. As long as I have Gabe, I can live with anything.

"I know something's wrong," I say as I steer the car down back roads, instinctively guiding us toward the highway, not caring where we're spit out. I know the area around here well enough to get us home in minutes as soon as I see a mile marker. "But I want you to know that I'm not going anywhere. I want to help, no matter what it takes."

Gabe sighs. "Okay."

I blink, and cast him a surprised glance out of the corner of my eye. "That's it?"

"I was expecting you'd say that, and I know how strong and determined you are. I knew it when I was driving to your house tonight, but now…" He looks over at me, admiration in his eyes. "Now, I wouldn't put anything past you. You were amazing. I'm proud of you and I love you so much."

Tears fill my eyes, but I bite my lip, using the pain to hold them at bay. "I love you, too. But don't ever try to get rid of me again, okay? I can handle anything, but that."

"I won't," Gabe says. "And I won't leave. At least not willingly, I promise."

I sniff away the stinging in my eyes, swiping the back of my hand across my nose. "What should I do with these clothes?" I ask, not wanting to think about the last thing he said, or what might be so wrong with him that he felt compelled to try to destroy us in order to shelter me from it.

Better to concentrate on the things I can control, at least until we're back at the house.

"I'll take them home and burn them in the back forty tomorrow," Gabe says. "The police shouldn't have any reason to come to your house tonight, but even if they did, I pulled those from Pitt's clean laundry. They shouldn't have any DNA or anything on them that would connect them to him or that house."

I nod, feeling a little of the tension leak from my arms. "Okay."

We drive in silence for a few minutes, before Gabe softly asks. "Can I ask a favor?"

"Anything," I say, meaning it. I would do anything for him, and I know he would do anything for me.

"Can we wait to talk until tomorrow morning? I want one more night. I just want to hold you and go to sleep with you on my chest and pretend that everything is the same. Just for one more night."

My tongue slips out to dampen my lips and tears are slipping down my cheeks again, but I nod. "But tomorrow you tell me the truth, and we move forward. Together."

"Yes. Together." He reaches out, threading his fingers through mine. "I don't want you to feel guilty about what happened tonight, okay? We didn't have a choice. If he'd lived, he would have continued to be a danger to you and the kids. Even if I could have convinced him to leave you alone, he'd obviously developed a taste for what he did to his mother. He would have found another victim, sooner or later."

I slow, braking as we pass under the overpass and prepare to turn south on the highway. "I don't feel guilty." I stop in the middle of the abandoned road, and turn to face him. "Do you think that makes me one of them?"

"One of the monsters?" Gabe asks, reading my mind the way he does sometimes. "No. Not even close."

"Are you sure?" I ask, suddenly needing the assurance, making me wonder if maybe I am in shock, after all, and if any minute my fragile calm is going to come crashing down all around me.

"No, you're an angel, the scary, beautiful kind," he says, lifting his hand to my face, cupping my cheek in his warm palm. "You are...the most beautiful person I've ever met, inside and out. I love you, and I wouldn't have you any other way than the way you were tonight."

Tears slip from my eyes. "Is it okay that that's enough for me?"

"Yes," he says with such surety that I'm able to pull myself together with only a nod and another sniff.

We drive home in silence to find Danny sitting on the front porch with one of the pay-as-you-go cell phones Gabe bought under an alias clenched tight in his hand. Even in the heat of the moment, Gabe was careful to make sure the call to the police wouldn't lead back to our family, and Danny was level-headed enough to follow directions.

Or crazy enough. I can tell Danny realizes something bad went down, but he doesn't ask any questions. He just throws his thin arms around me and hugs me tight before doing the same to Gabe.

I look over to see Gabe's big arms cradling my

44

brother to his chest and I have an eerie feeling that Danny is like me, like Gabe, that whatever is missing inside of us is missing from Danny, too, but it doesn't scare me the way it would have even a month ago.

Maybe more people are missing whatever this is than we think. Maybe other people aren't near as good or pure or kind as they would like to believe. Maybe Gabe was right that first night in Sherry's car, and none of us truly know what we're capable of until we're put in an impossible situation, until we step over the line and realize things aren't so very different on the other side, after all.

Whatever the truth is, I know Danny will be okay. He has me, and he has Gabe, and we'll help him figure out how to walk a path that is good and honorable, even if it isn't always a path other people would approve of. It can be done; I believe that. Anything can be done with people who love you by your side.

Half an hour later, it is almost three o'clock in the morning and Danny is tucked back into bed and I take Gabe's hand and let him lead me into the bathroom to wash away the stains of the day, to spend one last night letting all the questions lie before the sun rises and exposes all our secrets to the light.

CHAPTER FOUR

GABE

Let me not to the marriage of true minds
Admit impediments. Love is not love
Which alters when it alteration finds,
Or bends with the remover to remove:
O no; it is an ever-fixed mark,
That looks on tempests, and is never shaken.
-Shakespeare

*S*he's still crying, though I'm not sure she realizes it.

Tears stream soundlessly from her eyes, like a leaky faucet that refuses to be turned all the way off. There have been times when the tears have been worse than others, but they haven't really stopped since we left Pitt's house.

She says she's okay, but I can tell she's not.

And why should she be? She was almost killed, maybe almost raped, too—I haven't worked up the courage to ask her about that. I don't want to know. I'm afraid it would make my head start exploding all over again.

Stress seems to play a role in the blackouts and dizziness. If I want to be here for Caitlin tonight, I have to remain calm, and hold my shit together. I can't think about the fact that I'm dying, or that I'm going to leave her alone to carry the weight of what happened tonight all on her own. I can't think about Danny's thin arms trying to gather Caitlin up and hold her together. No matter how tough he is, he's just a kid. He clung to me tonight like I was his dad, not some idiot barely eight years older than he is.

Standing there on the porch, that kid clinging to me like I was the only thing standing between him and losing everything he cares about, I realized how deeply I've fucked things up. I have fucked them up so badly I don't know how to start making them right, but I'll start here, now, with Caitlin. By finding a way to help her stop crying.

I draw a bath in the chipped claw foot tub while she sits on the toilet, watching me with her red-rimmed, shell-shocked eyes, then I help her out of her clothes and into the hot water. Like earlier tonight, when she was walking around Pitt's attic wearing nothing but black bikini panties, her nakedness doesn't affect me the way it usually would. Now, it only makes me more keenly aware of how vulnerable she is, how easy it would be for someone to hurt her, no matter how strong she is, or how well she held it together while we were cleaning up after the killing.

Killing. We killed a man. Together.

It hits me like a slap in the face every time the thought drifts through my mind.

I never dreamt things would go this far, I never intended to lead Caitlin to such a dark place, but I don't regret it. Pitt had to die. If he'd lived, I would never have been able to trust that Caitlin was safe. I just wish I'd been able to finish the job, that another mind-blowing episode of vertigo and pain hadn't hit at the wrong time and left Caitlin to pick up where I left off.

I will never forget the way she looked, the intensity and agony and determination mixing on her face as she straddled Pitt and locked her hands around his throat. She was different after, transformed. I can't put my finger on what it is, but something was born inside her when Pitt died, something savage and raw I can sense humming in her bones as I brush a washcloth over her back, washing away the soap clinging to her skin.

"Do you want to talk about it?" I reach for the soap again and draw one of her legs from the water. I start with her toes, lathering each one before moving up to her calf and knee, finding it soothing to do this for her. To take care of her, even in this small way.

She leans back in the tub, the hair hanging loose below her shoulders turning into darker tendrils of blond as she sinks lower in the water. "What's there to talk about?"

"The fact that you can't stop crying," I say in a gentle voice, easing the leg I'm holding beneath the water and reaching for her other foot.

Caitlin lifts her hands, swiping her palms across her cheeks. "Oh." She sniffs, blinks, and after a moment the tears finally stop. "There. All better."

"I highly doubt that," I say. "It's been a rough night, to say the least."

Caitlin huffs, a sound that is almost a laugh, but not. "You think?" She sighs, leaning her head back on the edge of the tub, staring up at the ceiling. "You know the worst part?"

"What's that?"

"I wouldn't go back and undo it, even if I could," she says, eyes still flicking back and forth across the ceiling, as if reading some great truth on the water-stained paint.

"You shouldn't," I say, massaging her calf. "Like I said before, he had to die, or you and the kids would never have been safe."

"No, I don't mean that." She drops her gaze, staring into me with such a naked look I forget what I'm doing, forget everything but this girl, *my* girl, who is such a part of me her emotions echo inside my chest. "I mean us. Everything we've done. I wouldn't take any of it back. I wouldn't give up a moment with you, even if it could keep tonight from happening."

Tears well in her eyes again, but they don't spill over, even when her lips pull into the saddest smile I've ever seen. "But I'm afraid, Gabe. I'm so afraid. I know we promised to have one more night, but I can't stop thinking... I can't stop worrying. I can't lose you, I just can't. I don't know who I am without you anymore."

I swallow and it hurts like hell, like I'm swallowing a strawberry stuffed with razorblades, forcing it down whole.

But that's good. That's what I deserve. I deserve pain. I deserve to suffer for how epically stupid I've been.

"I never meant for this to happen," I say, my throat clenching so tight it feels like the muscles in my neck are going to snap. "I didn't think feelings like this existed. I'd never been in love and I never imagined… I never meant to get so lost in you, and I certainly never meant for you to get so lost in me."

"I'm not lost," she says, sitting up, cupping my face in her damp hands. "I'm found. In you. In us."

I hold her gaze, unable to speak for fear I'll start crying and never stop. I haven't cried once since March, not a single time since the morning the doctor told me the hellish headaches I'd been having were caused by a tumor in my frontal lobe, a malignant monster with tentacles spreading out into the parietal and occipital lobes, ensuring surgery would be a roll of the dice with the odds not at all in my favor.

I didn't see the point in weeping like a baby over something I couldn't change. But back then I didn't have near as much to live for.

I didn't have love; I didn't have her.

"You helped me find myself," Caitlin continues, thumb brushing lightly across my lips. "I was so afraid of turning out like my parents that I spent all my time trying *not* to be like them, instead of trying to be me. I had no idea who I really was until you walked up to me on the dance floor and put all of this in motion, and I am grateful to you for that. No matter what."

I press my lips together, teeth biting into my

flesh, fighting for control before I speak. "Even if I'm a liar?"

"Even if you're a liar," she says, fresh tears sliding down her pale cheeks. "As long as you didn't lie about loving me."

"Never." I choke on the word and lose the battle with the stinging in my eyes. "I love you so much. I love you more than anything, but I'm going to hurt you, Caitlin."

"Stop," she whispers, pulling me closer, pressing a kiss to my cheek.

"I never meant to." I thread my fingers through her hair, pulling her close, gluing her forehead to mine, wishing she could absorb everything I'm thinking and feeling, that she could know without me speaking another word how much she means to me.

She is everything, and I would live for her if I could. I would walk through fire for her. I would face every fear, stand by her side through everything life would throw at us, because I would know I'd never find a better partner than this girl. This woman.

And she could have been mine. She could have been mine, and it shatters what's left of my heart to know we have so little time left.

"I thought it would all be okay," I say, pulling away to look into her sad green eyes. "I thought we could have some fun, do some good, and walk away without getting hurt, but I'm a fucking idiot and I hate myself for it. And I'm sorry, but I know sorry will never be good enough to make up for what I've done."

She shakes her head. "Just tell me, Gabe. I can't take the not knowing anymore. Are you sick? Is that it?"

I bury my face in my hands, wishing I could keep up the lie, and spare her this for another day, but I can't. She deserves the truth. She deserves better than the truth, but at least I can give her that.

I lift my head, feeling like a balloon with all the air leaking away. It all comes out—the tumor, the large size and troubling shape, the location that makes it impossible to operate without shredding my memories, my personality, maybe everything that makes me who I am. I tell her about the decision not to operate, but to accept my six months to a year and make the most of them. I tell her about the hospice reservations my mother made today, and the plane flight I'm supposed to take the morning after next.

"But I'll stay if you want me to," I say, the urge to cry vanished, replaced by a massive hollow feeling. I'm a pillar of ash, all my life nearly burned away. All it will take is a strong wind to scatter what's left of me to the far reaches of the earth.

Caitlin watches me with a strangely calm expression, but her eyes are dry now, too, and I can see the wheels turning in her mind. "What about the surgery?" she asks. "Why not try it now?"

I shake my head. "The chances of survival aren't even fifty-fifty. The doctor gave me a thirty percent chance, and that was back in March, before the tumor had more time to spread."

Caitlin's brow furrows. "So? Thirty is better than zero. Ten is better than zero. You have to at least try. You can't give up on us without a fight."

"I could be a vegetable, Caitlin. I could end up needing help pissing and shitting and rolling out of bed in the morning for the rest of my life," I say harshly, needing her to understand. "And even if there were a miracle and I made it through surgery relatively whole, I would lose huge chunks of my memories, my thoughts, my opinions. I wouldn't be the same person. I...I might not even love you anymore."

"So?" she says, but I can see the hope leaking from her expression. "Then I'd just have to make you fall in love with me all over again."

I smile even though it hurts. "Not if I'm not me. Not if I go back to being the same arrogant, self-involved asshole who sat behind you in study hall for a year in high school without realizing the most beautiful, fascinating person he's ever met was sitting three feet away."

Her face crumples, but she fights through the wave of emotion, sucking in a ragged breath as she shakes her head. "I won't believe there's no hope. I can't. There's still a chance, and if you love me the way you say you do, then you will fight for it. You told me that love like what I feel for the kids is worth fighting for. Love like what *we* have is worth fighting for, too. You know it is."

"I do. But what if I wake up from surgery with a memory of you choking the life out of Pitt, and no context to place it in?"

She pales and I know she's already traced that hypothetical to its logical conclusion.

"There are so many potentially dangerous memories inside me," I say. "And I don't know what kind of moral compass I'll wake up with. I could still be the same old me, or I could wake up a monochromatic person, with a black and white view of the world, who thinks anyone who steps outside the law should be punished."

"I would risk it," she says, lower lip trembling. "I'd rather be in prison, and know you're alive, than be free, and live without you."

"I love you too much to risk it," I say softly. "And I *like* who I am. The person I've become is important to me. I don't want to lose myself.

That's part of the reason I made the decision not to have the surgery in the first place."

She watches me for a long, silent moment, evidently reading the determination in my face. Finally, she sniffs, draws her knees to her chest, and drops her chin to rest on top. "Okay."

"Okay?"

"Cancel the flight," she whispers. "I want you to stay."

"Are you sure?" I ask, wanting her to know what she's signing up for. "It will probably be bad at the end. Maybe too much for you to handle alone."

"We'll hire a nurse if we have to," she says, still refusing to look at me. "I want you to stay. I want every minute I can get."

"I want that, too." I reach out, brushing her half-wet hair over her bare shoulder, needing to put this conversation away. "And right now I want to wash your hair. I've never washed a girl's hair."

She blinks and takes another deep breath before she stretches out her legs, lying back in the lightly soapy water, wetting the rest of her hair before sitting back up to lean against the side of the tub.

I fetch the sandalwood shampoo from the bottles in the basket latched onto the side of the tub, realizing as I remove the lid that it is the source of Caitlin's spicy, earthy smell. I spill a cool dollop of light brown liquid onto my palm and work it through her hair. I scrub every inch of her scalp, massage the tight muscles behind her ears and at the base of her skull, funneling all the love I feel for her into every touch, every caress.

I tell her with my hands that I never want to leave her, that I will love her forever, in whatever place I end up after my life is through, and by the time she dunks her head to wash away the shampoo, tears are streaming down her cheeks all over again.

"I wanted to help you stop crying," I say as she emerges, swiping soap and water from her face.

"You're really good at washing hair," she says, sniffing as she reaches down to pull the plug from the tub. "Like a professional."

"I could have made a career of it, you think?" I tease. "If the lawyer thing hadn't worked out, and I hadn't grown myself a tumor?"

She turns to me, the ravaged look on her face banishing my smile.

"I'm sorry," I whisper. "I'm an asshole."

"You *are* an asshole," she says as she reaches for me, snatching my face in her wet hands and pulling my lips to hers.

The kiss is desperate and hungry and sad, but it's hot, too. It's electric because Caitlin and I are electric together, no matter what the sad ass circumstances. In a moment, my blood is pumping faster, in two, my cock is rock hard and pulsing between my legs, dying to be inside her, to shove into her tight heat and lose myself in the woman I love.

"Bed," I mumble into her mouth as I pull her out of the bath and into my arms.

She wraps her arms around my neck and her legs around my waist and clings to me, dampening the front of my clothes with her fresh-from-the-bath body. She is hot and wet and smells like flowers and smoky spices and Caitlin, a potent combination that makes my head spin.

But it's a lustful head spin this time, and the pain and vertigo blessedly leave me the fuck alone as I snatch a towel from the overflowing door hanger and throw it around Caitlin, concealing her nakedness from any kids who might be wandering the halls as I carry her from the bathroom into her bedroom.

But as soon as the door shuts behind us, she squirms out of my arms, pulling me toward the bed, helping me strip out of my clothes with shaking hands. I can feel her desperation echoing through my bones, and I know this isn't going to be slow or sweet. This is going to be me and Caitlin, raw and hungry, affirming that we are still alive and still in love and neither death, nor murder, nor pain, nor anything else is going to steal that away from us.

Not yet. Not fucking yet.

I fall on top of her on the bed, swallowing her cry of need with another kiss as I spread her legs with a sharp nudge of my knees and guide my cock to her entrance. I shove inside, groaning at the feel of her body fighting me as I push through her only slightly damp outer folds, but then I reach the core of her and she is molten hot and wet and as crazy for me as I am for her.

She arches her back, taking me deeper, coating me with her slick heat and then I am gone. I am soaring above it all with the only girl who has ever made my blood rush like this, made my heart break open, and love I didn't know I was capable of come spilling out.

She is my match, my partner, and the only girl I will ever love for however much longer I will live.

CHAPTER FIVE

CAITLIN

People live in each other's shelter. –Irish proverb

He drives to the end of my unprepared body and it hurts, but only a little. It's not enough, not near as much as I want it to hurt. I want to be bruised by the force of our coming together. I want my body to feel as ravaged as my heart. I want to come screaming for mercy, not begging for release.

I dig my nails into his ass, forcing him deeper, faster, harder. I arch my back, shoving my hips into him until I start to feel sore and tender, and still I fight him for more. I score his skin with my nails, dig my teeth into his lip, his neck, the thick muscle of his bicep. I mark him, crying out in relief as he marks me back. His teeth dig into the sensitive skin between my neck and shoulder, and his fingers pinch my nipple hard enough for the sting to go rushing out along every nerve ending.

"Yes," I growl into his ear. "Harder. Fuck me like you mean it."

"I always fuck you like I mean it," he says, shifting the angle of his penetration until his cock rams even deeper inside me, the thick head of him slamming against the entrance to my womb, sending sharp waves of discomfort coursing through me with each battering thrust.

But I don't want discomfort. I want to hurt. I *need* to hurt.

"More," I beg, wrapping my legs around his waist and lifting my hips. "Fuck me, Gabe. Please, fuck me. Don't hold back, don't fucking hold back."

He grips my hips in his hands, taking control of my body, jerking me up and down his cock as he slams home again and again, taking me so hard and fast my breasts shake and my spine twinges from the reverberations of each brutal thrust. My jaw begins to ache and my temples pulse as every muscle in my body strains closer, closer, until I'm tearing at him with my nails, gritting my teeth against the dark wave of pleasure-pain rolling in to pull me under.

My orgasm slams into me with the force of a tsunami hitting shore. It is savage and cruel and beautiful, all at the same time. The pleasure is smothering, blinding. It sucks me down to the sea floor of myself, down into the utter blackness where there is no light, and no place to hide, and it is so cold and lonely there. It is barren and bleak and empty, a post-apocalyptic landscape where nothing will ever grow again.

No matter how fiercely I cling to Gabe as he loses himself inside me, down here, down at my very core, I've already let him go. He's already gone, already dead, and I am a shell of a person who will have to find some way to keep going without him.

"God, I can't," I whisper, tears streaming down my face for the thousandth time tonight. "I can't do this without you."

And then I am crying my eyes out again and Gabe is holding me close and whispering that he loves me and that he's sorry and that I'm beautiful and strong and he's going to make everything as easy for us both as he can. He doesn't promise everything will be okay; he doesn't say I'll be fine. He just keeps repeating that he loves me, and believes in me, and that he will love me forever.

"Forever," he whispers into my hair as he

cradles me close. "Until men are fairy tales, and the world goes up in a ball of fire."

Finally, his soft voice and his hands stroking my back—as gentle now as they were ruthless a few minutes ago—calm me. I curl into him, resting my cheek on his bare chest, holding him close. My hip muscles are sore and aching and the delicate tissue between my legs is so bruised I know I'll need to sit carefully tomorrow, but I'm glad. I will treasure this evidence that Gabe is real and alive and still with me, at least for a little longer. I wish I could keep these little hurts for the rest of my life, wish I could have proof of the man I love imprinted permanently on my body.

"I want to get a tattoo," I whisper against his skin, words slurred by the exhaustion pulling at the backs of my eyes. "Tomorrow. I want us to get one together."

"What do you want to get?" he asks, fingers trailing lightly up and down my arm.

"Dandelion seeds." I kiss his chest, and flick my tongue out along his sweat-damp skin, wanting the taste of Gabe in my mouth before I go to sleep. "Dandelion seeds blowing away in the wind."

He hums, vibrating my cheek. "Off in their different directions, but from the same source. Always a part of each other."

I smile even as pain tightens the skin between

my eyebrows. He understands. Of course he does. He always understands, in a way no one ever has, and no one else ever will.

"We'll go tomorrow," he says. "I know a good shop in Charleston. We can get tattoos and then go make another deposit in your account. I'm leaving you my trust fund—I've already had the will drawn up—but it might take time for the lawyers to sort that out after. I want to know you're taken care of until then."

"I don't want your trust fund," I say, knowing I'd start crying again if I had any tears left.

"Well, you're getting it, so suck it up, blondie," he says, making me smile.

"I love you," I whisper as I fall asleep.

"Forever," he says.

It is the last word I hear before I'm sucked into a cold, hopeless sleep, where no dream dares to tread.

CHAPTER SIX

CAITLIN

Health to the men, and may the women live forever. –
Irish toast

We don't wake up until ten, which is a minor miracle in itself. I can't remember the last time I slept this late. The kids usually would have made way too much noise for such a thing to be possible, but when I finally drag myself out of bed and head downstairs, I find all the Cooneys camped out on the couch watching *The Wizard of Oz*, one of the only movies that captivates both toddlers and big kids, alike.

Danny has made popcorn, and everyone is so

sucked in to the flying monkey scene they barely notice me padding down the stairs.

"I called the diner and said you were sick, then I called the daycare," Danny says, nodding in my direction with a casualness that belies how scared I know he was when Gabe and I came home early this morning. "I told them Emmie and Sean were both shitting all over the place, so we were all going to stay home until we weren't contagious."

I nod as I head toward the coffeemaker. "Good."

I'm too tired to get on to him about cussing, and who gives a shit, anyway. Let the kid cuss. Let him have his big bad words if it makes him feel powerful and in control. I have bigger problems than a brother with a colorful vocabulary, and so does the world.

"Danny, if I call Sherry to see if she can come help, can you help hold down the fort today while Gabe and I go take care of some errands?"

Danny shrugs. "Yeah, what are you going to go do?"

"Gabe's going to be moving in with us for a little while," I say, dumping water in the back of the coffeemaker and hitting the start button. "So we need to head into Charleston and put a few things in order."

"He is?" Ray asks, tearing his attention away

from the screen with a grin. "That's cool. When is he moving in?"

"Today." I focus on fetching mugs and milk and sugar, not wanting to make eye contact with my brothers. I'm going to have to sit everyone down and have a hard talk about what's happening to Gabe, and how we're going to help him, but not today. I'm not ready for a talk about death and pain and all the fucking unfairness of life, today. We'll have that talk later, when I've had time to pull myself together.

I grab my cell and call Sherry, who says she can be over in a couple of hours and will bring the slip 'n slide from her garage for the kids to play on. I thank her profusely, and promise to give her all the gossip on what's going on with me and Gabe at the earliest possible moment. She's so excited that he's moving in, I can't stand to tell her the reason just yet.

We hang up as the coffee maker is huffing and puffing out the final drops of coffee, and I focus on breakfast. Simple things, getting through the morning one step at a time. I toast bread and coat four slices with butter—figuring Gabe probably isn't up for a big breakfast any more than I am—pour two coffees, and take the tray back upstairs, surprised to find Gabe already mostly dressed and in the bathroom using my brush to tame his wild hair.

"Hey, beautiful," he says, smiling when our eyes meet in the mirror.

He looks so normal, so healthy and fine and like the old Gorgeous Gabe with trouble in his eyes. It's so hard to believe that he's dying, that in a few weeks—or months, if we're lucky—he won't be here anymore.

"I thought you were going to let me bring you breakfast in bed." I set the tray on the back of the toilet before moving into his open arms, pushing the heavy thoughts away. I can't think about it, I'm still too emotionally raw from everything that happened last night.

Last night, when we killed a man.

We killed a man, and Gabe is dying.

I feel like a character from one of those old cartoons, the ones where a one-ton anvil falls on someone's head, squashing them into the pavement. But I'm not squashed, I'm still walking around, making breakfast, hugging Gabe, going through the motions, numb and sad and scared, but still here, still ticking.

Tick tock, tick tock, like a bomb waiting to go off and wreck everything I touch, but I haven't yet. Maybe I never will...but I think it's too soon to tell.

"I realized I should head home first," Gabe says. "I'll go back to Darby Hill, tell my parents what's going on, pack a bag, and come right back."

"You could just call them," I say, arms tightening around his waist as I press my face to the soft fabric of his white undershirt and inhale his Gabe smell. "And we could buy you new things in Charleston. Sherry's coming in a couple hours to watch the kids, and I don't want you to leave."

Gabe kisses the top of my head. "I don't want to leave, but I have medicine there, too. Pain pills and meds that helps keep the symptoms under control."

Medicine. Symptoms. This is real. It is real, and it isn't going away.

I pull back with a sigh, nodding. "All right. But let's eat breakfast first, and then I can get dressed and drive you. I don't want you to have an accident."

"I won't," he says. "I'm feeling a lot better. The pain I've had the past few days is gone so…maybe I'm not going downhill as fast as I thought."

I take a breath. "Well, that's good." It *is* good. It means more time, and I'll take as much of that as I can get.

And maybe, just maybe, with more time, I can find a way to convince him to give the surgery a shot, no matter how set in stone he seemed on the subject last night. I understand why he made the decision he did, but I'm also greedy. I don't want Gabe for a few months; I want Gabe forever, for the rest of my life. I want to grow up with him, grow old with him, and have those babies I thought I'd be too tired to raise with the man I love.

We didn't use a condom last night. I didn't realize it until this morning, but I wasn't freaked out when I did. A part of me actually hopes I'm pregnant. A baby would be something else for Gabe to live for, and give me a piece of him to keep loving if the worst actually comes to pass.

"I'll be back before you know it." Gabe leans down, capturing my lips in a kiss that makes me tingle all over despite the dark thoughts tromping through my head. "And then we'll head into Charleston, get tattoos, get money, and treat the kids to a steak dinner at Roxie's on the Square when we get back."

"Roxie's?" I shake my head. "No way. That will cost a million dollars."

"Money is just money," he says. "I want to spend it."

"But don't they have a dress code? We can't take the kids there in stained tee shirts and jeans."

"We'll buy them khakis and polos in town today, and a new dress for Emmie," he says, grinning. "I want to see the Cooneys dressed up. I have a feeling y'all are going to clean up nice." He reaches down, squeezing my ass as he leans in to whisper his next words against my neck. "Especially this Cooney. I want to see you in something black and slinky with no shoulders."

My eyes slide closed as I lean into him. "All right, but if the kids act like savages, don't blame me. They've never been to a sit down restaurant before."

"Well, they'll have to get used to it," he says, kissing my lips one last time before he pulls away to finish up with his hair. "Because I'm taking you all out at least once a week, and I don't want to hear any complaints."

"Yes, sir," I say, with a mock salute.

His eyes darken as our gazes connect in the mirror. "And we'll do more of that, too. I want to play games with you. I've been fantasizing about you tying me up since the night we danced together."

"Oh yeah?" I ask, lifting a brow. "I would have thought you'd prefer *I* be the one tied up."

"You'll be tied up first," he says, as if that's only logical. "But then I'll take my turn. I want you to make me beg for it." He sets the brush down and turns, crossing his arms as he leans back against the sink and surveys me with a predatory look. "I want to watch your breasts bounce while you ride me and suffer the torture of knowing I can't get my mouth on them unless you let me."

My tongue slips out to wet my lips. "If you

keep talking like that, we're heading back into the bedroom and those clothes are coming right back off."

He grins. "As lovely as that threat sounds, I'd rather get this business with the parents behind me. I have a feeling they're not going to be happy."

"You think it will be a bad scene?" I ask. "Do you want me to come with you?"

He shakes his head. "No. I want you to stay here, have coffee, hang out with the kids, and enjoy the rest of your morning. You've been through enough the past two days. From here on out, any way I can spare you more of that, I will."

"You don't have to spare me," I say. "I'm tougher than I look."

"Don't I know it." He kisses me again, a sweet kiss that feels like the sun on my face, before he whispers against my lips, "Be back in half an hour."

"Okay, love you."

"Love you," he says, and it sounds like the most natural, perfect thing in the world. I have no reason to doubt him, or his love. No reason at all.

And then twelve o'clock comes and goes and there's no sign of Gabe. I don't call—figuring he's probably in the middle of something with his mom and dad and not wanting to interrupt—but then Sherry arrives at one o'clock and I decide the phone call can't wait any longer, not if we want to have time to get everything done in Charleston before dinner.

I call Gabe's phone, but am sent directly to voice mail. It makes sense that he might turn his phone off before going to talk to his parents, but it doesn't make sense that he would keep me waiting for hours without at least texting to let me know that he's been delayed. Something is wrong, and after all we've been through I can't sit around and wait to see what's gone to shit this time. I have to take action.

I have to go to Darby Hill.

CHAPTER SEVEN

CAITLIN

I hug Sherry and the kids and tell them I'll be back soon and jump in the family van, rolling down the windows to let the hot summer air rush through as I head out into the country.

The sun is shining bright and the fields alongside of the road are green and ridiculously lush. Upcountry South Carolina looks like the best, prettiest, postcard version of itself, and I can't help but feel lifted up by the sight of it, by the smells of summer weeds and flowers floating in on the breeze, by the sounds of insects cricking and birds singing and all the trappings of summer that insist the world is alive. It is wild and alive and death won't dare lay a finger on anything right now, not while summer is here, wrapping the world in heat and abundance.

I hold on to my hope that there's been some simple glitch—Gabe's phone died, or his car broke down, or his parents put up more of a fight over the move than we anticipated—until I reach Darby Hill and see Gabe's parking spot in front of the azalea bushes empty.

I slam out of the van, heart beating in my throat as I start toward the front steps of the house, but before I can reach the veranda, Deborah opens the door. Her cheeks are red and blotchy and wet, but she isn't crying, and she doesn't say a word when I step onto the porch and ask her if she's okay.

She simply stares at me with this strange empty, lost expression for a long, long minute, a tense, strained, terrible minute that makes me feel like I'm going to lose my coffee and toast right there on her elegant doormat.

"What's wrong?" I ask, when the silence gets to be too much. "Has Gabe been here? He said he was coming to talk to you and Mr. Alexander."

"He was here," she says in a flat tone. "Here and gone."

"What do you mean?" I ask. "Where did he go?"

"Aaron came home for lunch and found Gabe passed out behind the wheel at the end of the drive," she says calmly. "It looks like he lost consciousness right after he made the turn."

My hand flies to cover my mouth, and my stomach cramps tighter, forming a sick knot at the center of me. This is my fault. I shouldn't have taken no for an answer. I should have made him let me drive him.

"Is he okay?" I finally ask. "Can I see him?"

Deborah licks her lips, and swipes an invisible hair behind her ear, taking what feels like an eternity before she answers. "Aaron took Gabe to the hospital, while I called our friend Mary, who works in emergency. She had everything ready for them when they arrived. She promised me it would be fine."

I nod, fighting to swallow past the lump in my throat. "So is he okay? Have you heard from the hospital? Can we go see him?"

She lifts her right hand, revealing a black cordless phone I hadn't realized she was holding. "Aaron called ten minutes ago. I thought he was going to tell me they were coming home."

I shake my head, feeling the truth bearing down on me like a runaway train, but I don't want to believe it. Gabe was fine just a few hours ago; he was better. He said he felt great. I don't want to accept what I know is coming, don't want to hear Deborah say another word. But I can't stop her. I can't stop her any more than I can stop autumn from coming, or death from putting his fingers wherever he likes, whenever he likes, even all over this perfect summer day.

"He's dead," Deborah says, brow wrinkling delicately as fresh tears fill her eyes. "My boy is dead. It's too late."

Her words hit me in my core, in my gut and my heart and every part of me that has lived harder since Gabe came into my life. They hit and a second later my knees hit the hard wooden boards beneath me, but I don't feel that pain. That pain is too small to register now that my entire world has become pain. There is nothing left to breathe but pain, not a shred of hope or light anywhere to be found.

I rock back and forth on my knees, arms wrapped tight around my shoulders, fighting for breath, too fucked up even to cry. I open my mouth to scream, but no sound comes out. My cry is wordless, soundless, a miserable silent wail that only the banshees can hear.

My grandma used to tell me stories about banshees before she died. She was first generation Irish, and still had so many beautiful, dark, mysterious stories to tell. She was the first magical person I ever met in my life. Gabe was the second.

And now they're both gone. Forever.

Forever. He promised to love me forever. Somewhere out there, wherever he is, he is still loving me, I know it. It isn't enough to banish the pain—not even close—but it helps me pull in a breath, and then another, and finally the tears break through and begin to fall.

I cry and cry. I have no idea how long, but gradually I become aware of the fact that Deborah is still standing in front of me. I look up, to find her staring down at me with an expression of such contempt that it makes me flinch.

"It's your fault," she says. "You were supposed to make him want to fight, want to *live*. You were supposed to convince him to have the surgery."

"I…I didn't even k-know," I stutter. "Not until y-yesterday."

"How could you not know?" she asks, eyes flying wide. "It was there, every day, every word he spoke, every time he did something the old Gabe would never have done. He wasn't the same. That thing in his head changed him, made him ruthless and cold and…" She shakes her head and her lip curls. "But you wouldn't know. You didn't know who he really was."

I stumble to my feet, so shocked it feels like the ground is tilting beneath me. "You're wrong. I knew him, and I loved him. I would have tried to—"

"You didn't know him, you knew the disease," she says, cutting me off. "And I should have known better than to think a girl in love with the heartless person Gabe had become could ever help me get my son back. I should have kicked you back to the hole you live in the second you darkened my door."

My jaw clenches, and anger boils inside me, but not for myself. "Gabe was anything but cold or heartless. He loved me, and he loved my brothers and Emmie, and he was a good, *good* man. He would have given his life for me, or any one of the kids." Tears fill my eyes, but I refuse to cry in front of this woman again. "If he was cold to you, maybe that's because *you're* cold, and he was tired of wasting his time on someone too stupid to see what a wonderful person he was."

"Get out," Deborah says, tears flowing down her cheeks.

"He told me how alone he was growing up," I say, unable to stop defending Gabe now that I've started. "How you couldn't even be bothered to tuck him into bed, and instead had the woman you hired to raise your son do it. How you made him feel like he was something to manage, not a person who deserved to be loved."

"Get out!" Deborah shouts, the words ending in a sob. "Or I'm calling the police."

"Fine," I shout back. "There's nothing here worth staying for anymore anyway."

I turn and charge back down the stairs and across the driveway. I slam into the van, and I drive back toward town. I force myself to go the speed limit. I force myself to pull over and check directions to the tattoo parlor on the edge of town on my phone instead of tapping letters into the search engine while I'm driving.

I keep my tears at bay for the next hour and a half as I find the tattoo parlor, give the artist the picture of the windblown dandelion that I picked out online this morning, and sit down in his chair to have the tattoo inked into my shoulder.

The pain of the needle dragging across my skin helps me stay present. I focus only on the moment, and how good it feels to be going through with this, to have the tattoo Gabe and I talked about on me. Forever. A permanent reminder of our love, and the summer that taught me to never take any beautiful thing for granted.

I force myself to hold it together until I've paid the artist, driven home, and have the van parked in the driveway. Only then do I turn off the ignition, drop my head to the wheel, and cry like the world is ending. Because it is. Part of it. A beautiful part I'm going to miss so much it feels like something vital has been removed from my body, leaving a toxic, hollow place behind.

I cry and cry, until my face is covered in tears

that drip down onto the bare skin below my shorts, taking the time to grieve Gabe alone before I go inside and tell the kids that someone they loved is gone.

CHAPTER EIGHT

CAITLIN

Death leaves a heartache no one can heal,
Love leaves a memory no one can steal. –Irish
headstone

Sherry stays the night, and the next day. We call in sick to work, call the kids in sick to daycare again, and make a gigantic pillow and sheet fort in the living room. All day Tuesday, we hide out in our fort, play board games, and watch our favorite movies. I take breaks to cry, but manage to hold myself together…mostly. Sherry helps, distracting the kids when I start to tear up, and need to make a run to the upstairs bathroom to hide.

By Tuesday night, the news that Mr. Pitt

committed suicide by setting himself on fire is all over the news. Sherry, Danny, and I watch the coverage on the tiny television in the kitchen, while the little kids are finishing their ice cream in the fort. I wash dishes, Danny dries, and Sherry stacks everything back onto the shelves. Sherry almost drops a plate when she hears Pitt left a suicide note confessing he murdered his mother—she had him for seventh grade, too, and has no trouble believing he was a psychopath. She makes it clear she isn't sorry to hear Pitt has checked himself out, but Danny doesn't say a word.

Our eyes meet as I pass him a salad bowl, he lifts one eyebrow, and I look away. And that's the end of it. We move on without another word about Pitt, the memories of that horrible night eclipsed by the greater grief of losing Gabe.

We wake up Wednesday morning to a gray day with rain pouring down, turning the front yard into a mud pit, and decide to call in sick again. We make cookies and run the air conditioner and play the longest game of Go Fish ever. We eat the pizzas Isaac brings over—all four of them—and make alligator puppets out of the boxes.

Isaac doesn't come in, but he gives me a hug that feels like one of his old hugs, and when he says he's sorry for my loss, I believe him. He tells me he talked to my dad again, and gives me a note from Chuck, written on one of the napkins from the restaurant.

I take it reluctantly, but when I start to read, Dad's message isn't what I expected.

Isaac told me about your boyfriend. I'm sorry, Kit Cat. I really am. It was obvious the boy cared about you, and no one should have to lose the person they love so young.

I've been thinking about you a lot these past weeks, wishing things could have been different. But I can't go back. None of us can.

I'm not going to fight you for the kids. You can have everything you asked for, just please let me see them. When I'm sober, and proven I deserve it.

I love you, and I'm sorry for all the times I've let you down.

Chuck

"I think he means it," I mumble before stuffing the napkin in the pocket of my brown pajama pants.

"I know you weren't talking to me," Isaac says, looking up at me from the bottom of the concrete steps outside the front door. "But I think he does, too. I think you finally got through to him."

I shrug, looking up at the gray sky and a darker gray cloud rolling in from the west, promising more rain. "For a little while, maybe.

He's had good times before, but the bad times always come back around."

"Well, at least you'll have custody of the kids when they do."

I nod. "Tell Chuck thanks for the note, and that I'll call him next week and we can go file the paperwork together. No need to keep the lawyers involved if he wants to do this the easy way."

"Will do," Isaac says, looking relieved.

I can tell he thinks the old Caitlin is back, ready to do the right thing, but I'm simply cutting my losses. I doubt Mr. Alexander is going to continue to represent me now that Gabe's dead and Deborah hates me, and I don't want to waste any of the stash Gabe and I put away on lawyers. He wouldn't want that.

"Should I bring more pizza by tomorrow?" Isaac asks. "I can bring veggie with no cheese and extra side salads, keep it healthy."

"Thanks," I say. "That would be really nice."

"See you at six tomorrow," he says with a smile before lifting one big hand in the air and starting back across the muddy yard to his truck.

I slip back inside and crawl back into the fort, cuddling under a blanket with Emmie while we watch the end of *Willie Wonka and the Chocolate Factory*.

We stay in our pajamas for over forty-eight hours before dragging ourselves upstairs to take a shower and change into fresh pajamas. Wednesday night, we go to bed in a giant puppy pile of pillows and sleeping bags inside the blanket fort. We tell ghost stories and jokes and we talk more about Gabe. I cry and so do Ray and Sean—and Emmie, because we're crying. I don't think she understands that Gabe's never coming back—but we laugh, too.

It feels good to remember Gabe, and to hear what the kids remember. He touched their lives this summer. Danny, Ray, Sean, and Emmie all cared about him, because *he* cared, and made them feel special, valuable.

Hearing the kids talk about their summer memories makes me even more certain that Gabe's mother is crazy. Gabe wasn't damaged by his disease; he was freed by it. He was freed to be the person he wanted to be, and I, for one, think that person was pretty fucking amazing.

He changed my life, and I will never be the same. I am stronger than I have ever been, and I have Gabe to thank for it. I won't let him down by falling apart or giving up on the dreams he helped me dream. I will hide until I'm healed enough to face the world, and then I'll start making the kind of decisions the man I loved would have been proud of.

By the time Sherry wakes me up on Thursday morning with a gentle shake to the shoulder, I'm feeling better, strong enough to nod yes when she asks if we can leave the fort and have a talk.

I follow her into the backyard, clutching the coffee mug she hands me to my chest. We walk bare foot across the still rain-soaked grass to the picnic table, where we both climb on top to sit with our grass-covered feet propped on the seat below.

"What's up?" I ask, shoving my wild hair from my face, deciding I'm ready to do something to it today besides wash it and let it dry in a tangle. I'm still not up for going to work, but I'm ready to get cleaned up, leave the fort, maybe take the kids to the playground later after things have dried off.

"I did a little calling around this morning," Sherry says. Her curly red hair is pulled into two cute braids and her pajamas are bright pink with green flowers. She looks like she's getting ready to host a kid's birthday party, but her expression is anything but cheerful, making me wonder what shit has hit the fan now.

"What's up?" I ask. "What kind of calling?"

"Well, it's been two days so I thought…" She takes a breath. "I figured it was time to call around to the funeral homes, and try to figure out when Gabe was going to be buried. I figured you'd want to know, so you could make plans."

I nod, handling the news much better than I

would have two days ago. The flash of pain in my chest is terrible, but duller around the edges, and when I speak my voice is rough, but steady. "Did you find out when it will be?"

Sherry shakes her head. "No. None of the funeral directors in town had a funeral scheduled, or had even heard from Gabe's parents."

I frown. "What does that mean? They can't be burying him somewhere else. His entire family back to the Civil War is buried in Giffney."

"Right," Sherry agrees, that odd, serious-nervous expression still on her face. "I thought that was weird, too, but thought maybe they were planning to hold the funeral in Charleston just to be assholes, and try to keep you from coming. So I called the local hospitals to see if they might be able to tell me where they released the body, but..."

She breaks off with a sigh.

"What?" I ask, stomach churning. "What's up? Just tell me."

Sherry takes my coffee and sets it on the table before grabbing both my hands and holding tight. "Listen, I don't want you to freak out, okay? And I don't want you to get your hopes up, because this probably doesn't mean anything, but—"

"But what?" I ask, pulse speeding. "What's wrong? Did they lose the body or something?"

Sherry shakes her head. "No, Caitlin. Gabe was never at the ER at Presbyterian."

My brow furrows, the sentence not computing. "What?"

"He was never there," she repeats. "So I called the Carolina Medical Center, even though it's further from Gabe's house, but he was never checked in there, either."

I stare at Sherry, watching the same impossible hope blooming in my chest flicker in her eyes. "You don't think…" I dampen my lips, afraid to say the words out loud. "We should check the Charleston hospitals first, before we start jumping to conclusions."

"I already did," Sherry says. "In the past four days, no Gabriel Alexander was checked in to *any* Emergency Room within two hours of Giffney."

I shake my head slowly back and forth, a million thoughts rushing through my mind at once. "You think he's… Do you think he…" I still can't say it, can't name my hope for fear it will disappear. "But why would his mom lie?"

"Why wouldn't she?" Sherry says. "You said she thought you weren't helping Gabe. Maybe she decided he was better off without you."

"But she was devastated," I say. "She was crying her eyes out."

"Maybe she's a really good liar. And I mean, her son *was* still dying, even if he wasn't dead yet.

That's something to fucking cry about." Sherry shrugs. "I don't know. It's all just too fishy, and didn't you say that Gabe said his parents had plane flights booked for him? To some hospice or something?"

I nod, still feeling dazed, blinded by the ray of light in the darkness.

"What if they kidnapped him?" Sherry continues. "Like, took advantage of the fact that he was sick, and put his ass on a plane as far from Giffney, and you, as they could get him?"

"No," I say, spirits crashing back to earth. "He would have found a phone and called me. Even if he was too sick to fight back, he wouldn't have let his parents take him away and not found a way to let me know about it."

"Unless he couldn't get to a phone for some reason," Sherry says, squeezing my hands tighter. "Listen, I don't want to put you through any fresh hell, or give you false hope, but there is something strange going on, and I'm going to help you figure out what it is. I already called Carla, and she told me to take the rest of the week off. She lost her husband last year. She told me to stay and be here for you, and that's what I'm going to do. So...where do we start digging for more clues?"

I take a shaky breath, hope and fear mixing inside of me to form a cocktail far more eye-opening than any cup of coffee. "There's only one place I can think of. I have to go back to Darby Hill. There might be something there that will let us know what Gabe's parents are hiding."

"Okay, but how?" Sherry asks, leaning in as she catches my excitement. "They're not going to throw open the door when you knock, and welcome you in for a chat."

"I'm not going to knock," I say. "I'll break in after they're asleep. I know the security code, so I can turn it off as soon as I pick the lock."

Sherry tilts her head, shooting me a confused look out of the corner of her eye. "Okay, but... when exactly did you become an expert at picking locks?"

"Gabe taught me," I say, shrugging like it's no big deal. "It was a hobby of his. He liked the... puzzle solving aspect of it."

"Really," she says, frowning. "That's...kind of a weird habit for a guy who's stinking rich. Was he planning a secret life of crime, or something?"

For the first time in days I actually have to fight a smile. On impulse I lean in, hugging Sherry tight. "Thank you. Thank you so much for this."

Sherry hugs me back, smoothing a hand over my tangled hair. "Just don't hate me if it turns out to be nothing, okay?"

"I could never hate you," I say, pulling away,

sniffing away the tears trying to escape the corners of my eyes. I'm not going to cry again, not until I know what's happened to Gabe, until I know if, by some miracle, he's still alive.

Gabe. Alive. The thought is a hand pulling me up from the bottom of the ocean. Even if he only has a little time left, I'll fight for every minute with him. I need to see him again, I need to know if—in two short weeks—my period comes, or if I find out there is a part of Gabe alive inside of me, a son or daughter with my green eyes and his devilish smile.

I take a moment, closing my eyes and praying for that potential life, praying for the life of the man I love, praying that I'll find him and be able to tell him I love him one more time. I love him, and I will never forget him. No matter what the future holds, a piece of Gabe will always be with me, burning hot and bright, lighting me up from the inside. He set fire to my heart, and there is no putting it out.

And if his parents have lied to take him away from me, there will be no stopping me until I have my revenge.

"You okay, Cait?" Sherry asks.

I open my eyes. "Not yet, but I will be."

I hop off the picnic table, leading the way back into the house, ready to set a few fires of my own.

CHAPTER NINE

CAITLIN

*"Parting is all we know of heaven
and all we need of hell."*
-Elizabeth Barrett Browning

*G*abe is alive. Gabe is alive. Gabe...

I know I may be fooling myself. There is probably a logical explanation as to why none of the funeral homes in town have received Gabe's body, and none of the hospitals near Giffney, South Carolina have treated a Gabe Alexander in the past few days. My head tells me the chances that the man I love is still alive are slim, at best, but my heart...

My heart is *on fire*.

I go through the motions of the day with hope

burning a hole in my chest. I help my best friend, Sherry, make my little brothers and niece breakfast with flames whispering against my ribs, making my blood burn and the mounting heat of the mid-summer day even harder to handle. I can't wait to go to Darby Hill tonight, to slip my lock pick into the servants' entrance door, and to tease the pins the way Gabe taught me, until the knob gives under my hand.

I feel like I'm only half in my body, the other half of me already tiptoeing through Gabe's parents' mansion. I help Danny and Ray clean up the blanket fort in the living room, but I don't see our shabby carpet or the couch that sags in the middle. I see priceless antiques and oil paintings, illuminated by yellow moonlight. I clean up the breakfast dishes with my mind racing, tracing the route I'll take up the servants' staircase to make sure Aaron and Deborah Alexander are sleeping in their bed before I start my investigation. I give Emmie a bath with my pulse fluttering wildly at my throat, as if I'm already sifting through Deborah's desk, looking for clues, not scrubbing toddler toes.

By the time I change Emmie into her favorite pink tee shirt, white bloomers, and rainbow tutu, my arms are trembling, and I know I need to calm down or I'll be exhausted before sunset.

"Play animals?" Emmie asks, pointing to the pile of stuffies on her toddler bed.

"Sure," I say, hoping it will help keep my mind off more dangerous subjects. But as I watch her skip across the room to grab her favorite stuffed koala, tutu bouncing around her waist, I can't help but think about the day Gabe bought the skirt for her at the French Heritage festival.

It was only a few weeks ago, but it feels like another lifetime. Back then, I had no idea the man I loved was living in the shadow of his own impending death, or that this summer would be the only one we'd ever have. It's only been *four* days since I learned that Gabe had chosen life on his own terms over the risky brain surgery that would ravage his memories and personality, even if he were lucky enough to beat the odds and come out alive. *Four* days since his mother told me that Gabe had died in the hospital. Four days I've lived with this shredded, ravaged feeling, like my soul has been sliced apart and left bleeding in the still, gray fog that is a world without Gabe.

Gabe. Gabe is alive. He has *to be alive.*

I have to see him one more time. I have to hold him, kiss his stubble-covered cheek, inhale the scent of his skin, and promise I will never forget. I have to swear to him that—if we made a child our last night together—I will love our son or daughter enough for both of us. Because Gabe loved me enough in six weeks to last a lifetime. I don't want to move on without him, but I can, and I will, if there is no other way.

But inside, I'm hoping for a miracle, praying with everything in me that I will find something in Gabe's parents' house that will prove his mother lied, and that the grief, that has threatened to devour me whole, can be put away. At least for a little while.

I need more time, if only to make sure I give the most important person in my life a proper goodbye.

"Do you need something?" Sherry asks later in the morning, nudging my hip with hers as we stand side by side at the kitchen counter making peanut butter sandwiches to take to the park.

"Like what?" I slap jelly on Ray's sandwich and reach for the honey for mine and Emmie's.

"Like a Xanax? Or a stiff drink? Your hands have been shaking all morning."

I let out an uneven breath, willing my arms to relax. "No. I'm good."

"Are you sure?"

I nod. "Yeah. I don't want to be out of it in the middle of the day."

And I don't want a sedative impairing my motor coordination. Gabe and I broke into half a dozen buildings together and I've practiced with his lock-picking tools enough that I'm quick with a simple mechanism, but I don't know what I'll be dealing with at Darby Hill. I never thought to check the locks on the servants' entrance door the few times Gabe and I had dinner with his parents.

"Remember, it could be nothing," Sherry cautions for at least the fifth time since she first told me that Gabe's body was nowhere to be found. "Someone could have made a mistake at the hospital, or I could have missed a funeral home, or—"

"You didn't."

"I know I didn't." She brushes her wild red curls from her forehead with a sigh, barely avoiding getting the peanut-butter-streaked knife in her hand stuck in her hair. "I'm just scared for you, C."

"Don't be scared. I know what I'm doing, and I have the security code memorized. I won't get caught."

"No, I mean..." Sherry casts a glance toward the living room where my twelve-year-old brother, Danny, is helping the little kids clean up toys, before turning back to me and continuing in a softer voice, "Are you going to be okay if it turns out Gabe's mom wasn't lying? If he really is...gone?"

I press my lips together and concentrate on cutting the sandwich in front of me into two perfect triangles, wondering how many peanut butter sandwiches I've made in my life. I'm doing the math—adding up the days since I took over raising my younger brothers and niece when I was seventeen, multiplying by three, and dividing by five to get an average of how many school lunches I've slapped together, anything to keep my mind off that awful question—when Sherry's fingers close around my wrist.

"Caitlin, seriously." She gives my arm a gentle squeeze before letting go. "If you fall apart at Gabe's house and get caught, his parents could call the cops. They could charge you with breaking and entering. You could go to jail, or at least have to pay a fine and—"

"I'm not going to fall apart," I say in an even tone. "I'm tougher than you think."

Sherry's brows draw together. "Well, I think you're a gladiator, so that's pretty tough."

I blink, surprised. I assumed no one but Gabe saw the strength in me.

"Don't look so shocked," she says, rolling her eyes. "I mean, for years you've been raising four kids all by yourself, working two jobs, and getting nothing but grief from your dad for your trouble. I would have cracked under the pressure the first day."

"No, you wouldn't."

Sherry's amber eyes go wide. "Oh, yes, I

would. The first time the kids all came down with the flu at the same time, I would have dissolved into a puddle of self-pity on the floor, and never gotten up again."

"You don't know what you're capable of until you're put in an impossible situation," I say, repeating the words Gabe said to me the night we pulled our first job.

Before this summer, I never would have dreamed I'd crave the rush of stealing from the people Gabe's father helped keep out of jail, balancing the scales of justice, while pulling my family out of poverty in the process. Before Gabe, I'd spent my life trying not to be like all the people who had let me down, instead of figuring out what I wanted from life. I hadn't known who I was, or what I was capable of.

Now, thanks to Gabe, I know that I am strong, and prepared to fight a hundred bloody battles if that's what it takes to find my way back to him. Less than a week ago, Gabe and I killed a man to protect the people we love. After that, a little breaking and entering is child's play.

Of course, Sherry doesn't know Gabe and I are responsible for Ned Pitt's death. No one except Danny even suspects, and that's the way it's going to stay. Sherry's right, I can't afford to go to prison. There's no one left to take care of my brothers and Emmie if I'm taken away. That's why I have to be careful, and make sure I don't get caught.

"You sure you're good with staying here tonight?" I ask, shoving the sandwich bags into our cracked wicker picnic basket, and adding a few apples from the bowl on the counter.

Sherry nods. "And if anyone asks, I'll swear you were asleep in the bed beside me, all night long."

"Don't worry about that," I say. "No one's going to—"

I'm interrupted by three loud raps at the back door. Even before the door slams open and my dad calls out—

"Who wants a lollipop?"

—I know it's Chuck.

My dad always comes in through the back door, like a thief in the night, taking the people unfortunate enough to be related to him by surprise.

CHAPTER TEN

CAITLIN

"We are sepulchered alive in this close world
And want more room."
-Elizabeth Barrett Browning

"*D*addy!" Sean dashes across the living room, jumping into Dad's arms as he enters the kitchen.

"Aw, there's my big man." Dad lifts Sean's feet off the floor, pulling my eight-year-old brother into a bear hug.

For once, Chuck looks relatively presentable. He's wearing wrinkled, but unstained, khaki shorts, new tennis shoes, and a light blue tee shirt the same color as his eyes that stretches tightly over his belly. His nose is bright red from a combination of sunburn and years of hard drinking, and his thinning salt and pepper hair is sticking up in ten different directions, but he's pulled together—for Chuck—and the usual cloud of alcohol fumes is noticeably absent.

My father is sober, clean, and has come bearing lollipops for the kids in one meaty hand. I suppose I should be happy he's making an effort, but I'm not. Chuck is the last person I want to see right now, when I'm so keyed up on impossible hope I can barely stand still.

Chuck is a hope killer, the one person in my life who has let me down more times than the rest of the world combined. He's been on his best behavior recently—promising to sign over custody of the kids, and part of his VA check, as long as I drop my lawsuit against him—but I still don't trust him. Years of suffering the slings and arrows of Chuck Cooney's drunk side, vengeful side, and plain nasty side have left me of the opinion that any day is better simply for *not* having any Chuck in it.

"What flavor do you want Long Sean Silver?" Dad asks as he sets Sean back on his feet, using one of the ridiculous pet names he has for all of his kids, the ones he thinks are valid substitutes for being a decent parent. "I've got three cherry, two blueberry, and a root beer. You gave the first hug, so you get first choice."

"Root beer!" Sean says before casting an uncertain glance my way. "Is that okay, Caitlin? Can I have it before lunch?"

"Sure." I force a smile that feels more like a baring of my teeth. "Just eat it at the table, okay?"

"Okay!" Sean runs off, grinning ear to ear, and Ray takes his place, giving Dad a slightly less enthusiastic hug before claiming two cherry lollipops—one for him, and one for Emmie, who he scoops up and settles in her high chair before handing over the candy.

"What about you, Danny Boy?" Dad comes to stand beside me and Sherry in the kitchen, smiling across the counter toward where Danny is slumped on the couch with a scowl on his face. "Cherry or blueberry?"

"No thanks," Danny grumbles, slouching lower. "I don't want your candy."

"Oh, come on," Chuck says. "You love lollipops."

"I said, I don't want your fucking candy!" Danny surges to his feet and bolts for the stairs, taking them two at a time, setting the house to shaking as he thunders up to his room and slams the door.

"Language!" Dad shouts after him, having the balls to put on his "you'd better behave" voice. Like he has the right to critique anyone's behavior when he's been drunk and belligerent for the better part of the past decade.

Chuck turns back to me, a concerned expression on his face. "He shouldn't be talking like that in front of the younger ones."

"You're right, Dad," I say, crossing my arms at my chest. "But I figure a big brother with a potty mouth who helps his little brothers with their homework is less of a problem than a Dad who shows up drunk and pukes on the supper table so..." I lift one shoulder and let it fall, holding my Dad's stare, even when hurt flickers in his eyes.

"I'm going to go...check on Danny," Sherry says as she backs out of the kitchen, obviously not inclined to get in the middle of the Cooney family drama.

"I'm not drunk today, Kit Cat," Dad says in a soft, wounded voice. "Doesn't seem fair to kick a man when he's trying his best to do better."

I suck at my teeth and press my tongue to the roof of my mouth, fighting to keep another smartass remark from my lips. Any man who has hit a twelve-year-old as many times as Dad has backhanded Danny, deserves to be kicked while he's down, but picking a fight with Chuck won't help anything. Right now, I need to play nice and get rid of him so I can keep my focus where it belongs—on finding out what happened to Gabe.

"Sorry." My tone is more begrudging than

penitent, but the apology seems to cheer Chuck. The hurt in his eyes fades as he unwraps a cherry lollipop, and holds it up between us. I take it and pop it into my mouth, figuring I can't say anything I'll regret if my mouth is full of candy.

"I remember when you were Sean's age," Chuck says with a fond smile. "You ate all your Halloween candy in one night and threw it up in the cat's litter box."

I scrunch my nose at the memory. "Gross, Dad. I'm eating."

"You were always eating when you were little," Chuck says, clearly determined to drag me down memory lane, kicking and screaming. "I used to think you'd end up three hundred pounds with a belly bigger than your old man's, but you stayed a bitty thing. Cute as a bug's ear, and nearly as tiny."

I force a smile and resist the urge to ask him what the fuck he wants. Chuck is rarely sweet when he doesn't want something. But he *is* sober, and he did bring candy for the kids. Maybe he's legitimately trying to be a decent dad and I should give him a chance to prove he isn't a complete waste.

No sooner has the thought passed through my head than Chuck leans in and says in a conspiratorial tone, "I've got something exciting to talk to you about, Kit Cat. A real opportunity. For all of us. A once-in-a-lifetime kind of opportunity."

I groan as I pull the lollipop from my mouth. "No way, Dad. I'm not interested."

His eyes widen. "You haven't even heard what I've got to say."

"I don't need to hear. The answer is no. The last time I let you talk me into one of your 'opportunities' I lost three hundred dollars."

"You didn't lose it, you invested it," Chuck says. "And if Dan hadn't given up two weeks in, we could have made the pyramid work. Those diet patches worked. I lost fifteen pounds without even switching to light beer."

"Like I said, I'm not interested," I repeat, the memory of how naïve I'd been, thinking handing money over to Chuck was a decent idea, making my cheeks heat with shame. "But thanks for coming by, and for bringing candy for the kids. That was nice."

I circle around him, dropping my unfinished lollipop in the trash, no longer able to tolerate the syrupy sweet taste of it any more than I can tolerate my father. I can't believe he's trying to sell me on one of his dumb schemes *four days* after my boyfriend passed away. Chuck doesn't know that there's a chance Gabe isn't dead. He thinks I've lost the only boy I ever loved. The note he sent over with Isaac made me think he understood how devastated I am, but apparently not.

Or maybe my dad figured I'd be over it by now. He was sleeping with two different women three days after his wife of sixteen years ran off with her AA sponsor. Maybe he thinks four days is plenty of time to mourn the loss of the love of your life.

"Hold on," Chuck says, reaching out to snag my elbow as I start into the living room.

I stiffen beneath his touch and am about to jerk my arm away when he releases me, lifting his hands up on either side of his head in a gesture of surrender.

"Don't be mad, Caity Did," he says. "I know I haven't been Father of the Year, but this is a real opportunity. I swear it to you. I just found out Great Aunt Sarah passed away a few months back. It took her attorneys some time to find me, but I got a letter yesterday. Turns out she left me *everything.*"

"Congratulations," I say, feeling sorry for Great Aunt Sarah, whoever she is. She must not have known Chuck very well, or she would have realized she was better off flushing her worldly possessions down the toilet than giving them to a man who pours every dime he has into wrecking his liver.

"Congratulations to *you,*" Chuck says, beaming. "I know I said I'd sign over the house here in Giffney to you, for you and the kids, but what would you say to a cottage on a tropical island, instead? I can keep the house here, and you and the kids can start a brand new adventure in paradise."

I let out a weary sigh, hoping I'm not going to have to hire a lawyer. I'm sure Gabe's dad, who was representing me for free, isn't going to be handling my custody case anymore. Whether Gabe's mom is lying about his death or not, something strange is going on with the Alexanders, and Deborah made it clear on her front porch the other day that she hates me.

No matter what happens, my days of free representation are over. With Chuck being so cooperative, I'd hoped I wouldn't have to find a new lawyer, but if he's trying to con me before my boyfriend's body is even in the ground, I was obviously mistaken.

"I say that sounds too good to be true," I say, unable to keep the sarcastic note from my voice. "I'm not a dumb kid anymore, Dad. I want what you promised me, and I want the paperwork filed by the end of the week. If you won't help me make that happen, we can keep the court date, and let the judge decide what's best for the kids."

"Now listen, Kit Cat, I—"

"I don't want to listen," I snap, temper flaring.

"Someone I loved more than anything in the world is dead, Dad. Can't you give me a break? Just for a few weeks?"

"I'm trying to give you a break. Please, just hear me out," Dad says, the desperate, pleading expression on his face making me nauseous.

He's pathetic. He is weak and broken and... rotten beneath the skin. There's something twisted up and wrong at the core of Chuck. Maybe, if he'd found something he could love more than alcohol, he would have still been a decent father, but he never loved his kids the way children are meant to be loved. He would never allow himself to be inconvenienced for any of us, let alone die for us.

I would give my life for my brothers or Emmie in a heartbeat. I would die for them, and maybe, more importantly, I have lived a life that is far from the life of my dreams because of the love I feel for them. I want them to have it better than I did growing up, and I'm willing to do whatever it takes to give them a stable childhood. I'm willing to lie, cheat, and steal; I'm willing to fight to my last breath, and waste precious money from the college fund Gabe helped me build to take my father to court, if that's what it takes. I'm done letting Chuck roll over me and crush everything good I try to build.

"I'm going to give you five minutes," I say in a

hard voice. "And then I want you to leave. If you refuse, I'm calling the police."

"All right, if that's the way you want it," Chuck says, the anger flashing in his eyes making him look more like the dad I'm used to, the one who is selfish to his last breath, and has no patience for people who refuse to give him what he wants. "I just thought you might be interested in a fresh start in a place where no one knows your dad's a drunk, your mom ran off, or your big sister was such a whore she had no clue which of the losers she'd slept with knocked her up."

"Hush," I hiss, casting a glance across the counter toward the kitchen table, where the kids are finishing up their lollipops. No one looks over, but I know Ray and Sean heard what Dad said, and I know Ray, at least, knows what "whore" means.

Thankfully, nearly three-year-old Emmie is too little to have any idea what Chuck's saying, and has no memory of her mother. My big sister, Aoife, left when Emmie was barely two months old, and hasn't sent so much as a Christmas card for her daughter since. For all intents and purposes, Emmie is my daughter, though she calls me Caitlin, like the rest of the kids.

I've done everything I can to shield Emmie from the negative parts of our family's history, but she will hear the gossip eventually. One day, she'll learn that she's "Easy Ee-fuh" Cooney's little girl. Maybe it will happen in elementary school, or maybe, if she's lucky, she'll stay under the bully radar until middle school. But there will come a day when Emmie will learn that her mom was a drug addict who spread her legs for anyone who promised her the escape she craved. She'll hear the nasty whispers around town, and probably end up being called a slut long before she has her first kiss, the way I was, simply because she's a Cooney and the latest in a long line of trash the people in this town expect only the worst from.

I would love to spare Emmie that pain and shame. I would love to give the boys a chance to grow up without the local police watching them like hawks, waiting for them to screw up, like their dad and granddad before them, but I know better than to trust Chuck. No matter how bright a picture he paints, there is always a dark, rancid lining to his shiny silver clouds.

Still, I promised him five minutes, and I do my best to keep my promises, unlike the man who raised me. "Fine, talk," I say, crossing my arms at my chest. "I'm listening."

I take the paperwork my father hands over, and give the pictures of the home he inherited from Great Aunt Sarah a cursory glance. The four-bedroom cottage in the tiny village of Haiku, on the island of Maui, is adorable. It has three bedrooms downstairs, and a large loft area overlooking the combination kitchen-and-living-room. It's situated on a two-acre parcel on a hill overlooking the ocean, and its lush, green yard is dotted with mango, orange, and avocado trees the real estate description promises are very productive.

It is beautiful, the perfect size for our family, and allegedly valued at over six-hundred thousand dollars.

CHAPTER ELEVEN

CAITLIN

*J*jab my finger at the number, running my nail beneath the digits to make sure I'm reading them correctly.

"This is worth six-hundred thousand dollars, Dad," I say, glancing up at him, expecting him to snatch the paper away and make a run for the back door.

He had to have missed the number. If not, he would have listed the house and pocketed the money. He would never give me a half a million dollar home in exchange for our house in Giffney, a house that probably wouldn't fetch more than one hundred and twenty thousand, even if I put on the new roof the repair guy insists is way overdue.

"I know." An impish smile crosses Chuck's face. "You kids will be living like movie stars. And there's a cottage at the back of the property, too. They call it an Ohana. The agent says it rents for eighteen hundred a month, which should cover a good chunk of your expenses. You'll be able to go back to working one job, Kit Cat, and have time for school. They've got a college on the island. It's supposed to be nice."

My eyes narrow as I search his face, looking for a fly in the ointment. "Why?"

"Why what?" Chuck asks, still grinning.

"Why would you give this to me? You could sell it and have more money than you've made in your entire life."

"I could," Chuck says, his expression sobering. "But we both know what I'd do with that much money. I can't be trusted with my monthly check. If I had more, I'd drink myself to death in a year. Maybe less."

My brows float higher on my forehead. Chuck has never talked to me like this before. He's never been honest about what a problem the drinking is. He's always said he has an Irish liver, or that the Cooneys can handle their booze better than anyone—like we're the superheroes of alcohol consumption—or he points out that his own father was drunk pretty much constantly from the age of fourteen, and lived to the ripe old age of seventy-eight. To hear him copping to the fact that the only thing keeping him from

126

drinking himself to death is a shortage of funds is surprising to say the least.

"And I like the idea of you kids living big because of me," Chuck says. "I never thought I'd be able to give you something like this, but now I can. It feels good. I want to put you all on a plane and wave good-bye, knowing you're going to a better life."

I study his face for a long moment, but he doesn't flinch or look away. He meets my eyes and holds my gaze.

If I didn't know better, I'd think he was a man who had nothing to hide, but I do know better. And so I look harder, past the sentimental expression, behind the soft blue eyes, down to the heart of my father, where there is nothing but Chuck looking out for Chuck, nothing but an overgrown child wailing and bargaining and snatching for the things he wants with his chubby hands.

Finally, I see it, that seed of self-interest, that tiny spark of gleeful satisfaction that Chuck gets when he's pulling one over on some unsuspecting soul.

He's up to something. I'd bet my college fund on it. I don't know what it is, but I'm not going to fall for this Repentant Father act, and I'm not getting on a plane to anywhere unless it's going to carry me closer to Gabe.

"That's sweet, Dad. I appreciate the offer," I say with my own saccharine smile, lies coming easier to me now than they did at the start of the summer. "Can I think about it for a while? It's been a hard few days."

"Of course it has, and it's a big change," Chuck says, nodding a little too fast. "But don't take too long. Aunt Sarah has her lawyers all paid up. They'll take care of everything if I tell them what to do in the next week or so. Otherwise, we'll have to pay someone else, and I don't have cash to spare."

"Okay, I'll let you know by next week," I say, knowing it's the quickest way to get rid of him. By next week, I'm hoping to be so busy taking care of Gabe I won't have time for Chuck's crap, but he doesn't need to know that. Not right now, anyway.

"Perfect." Chuck smiles a smile that is too bright for a man hoping to give away a six hundred thousand dollar home and pulls me in for a hug.

I go into his arms, forcing myself to soften against him, but when I lay my cheek against his chest all I feel is cold inside. Chuck's making a mistake if he thinks he can play me the way he has in the past. The sweet, gullible Caitlin, who secretly craved her father's love, is dead. She died that night in Pitt's attic, when I locked my fingers

128

around his throat and leaned all my weight forward, blocking off the air to his lungs, strangling the life out of the man who had kidnapped me. I'm someone different now, someone who watches the world with a calculated gaze, and who isn't afraid to play dirty to protect what is mine.

The kids are mine, and I won't let Chuck put their welfare in danger. They are mine the way Gabe is mine because I love them all with every cell in my body.

Gabe is imbedded in my heart, so much a part of me I swear I can still feel his soul whispering beneath my skin. I won't let his parents keep us apart. If he's still alive, I'm going to find him, and do whatever it takes to bring him back to me.

Gabe is alive, and I have to find him.

That's all I can think about now. There's no room for anything else, especially not my father's latest manipulations. I finish hugging Chuck good-bye and shoo him out the front door as quickly as possible, fifteen minutes with my father already more than I can tolerate.

As soon as Chuck disappears down the concrete steps, Ray pipes up from the kitchen table.

"You don't believe him, do you, Caitlin?" he asks, proving he was eavesdropping. "All of that sounds way too good to be true."

"I know, Ray," I say, ignoring the wave of sadness that rushes through my chest. I wish my brother was like any other ten-year-old kid, and could still believe in wonderful strokes of fortune, and magic, and fathers who come bearing gifts with no strings attached, but he's not. We all bear scars from the way we were raised, but those scars aren't wounds we should be ashamed of; they are marks earned in battle that have made us stronger, and better able to protect the people we love.

"I won't even consider taking him up on that offer until I've checked it out upside down and sideways," I say. "Don't worry. I've got your back."

"Me too," Ray says, with a smile. "I've got your back, too."

"I know you do." And even though a ten-year-old boy isn't the most intimidating ally in the world, at that moment, with Ray grinning at me with candy-sticky lips, Danny brooding upstairs, and Sean giggling as he bites into the last nub of his lollipop and half of it pops out onto the table, I feel lucky to have a few good, little men on my side.

CHAPTER TWELVE

CAITLIN

"Who so loves believes the impossible."
-Elizabeth Barrett Browning

I've never been afraid of the dark, not even when I was a little girl. The dark has always been a comforting place, a shadowy friend that keeps me safe from the scary things that live in lamp lit rooms.

When Aoife and I were little, before Danny was born, my parents went through one of the roughest times in their marriage. They were both young and angry—drinking too much, working too hard, sleeping too little, and blaming each other for the fact that none of their high school dreams were coming true. By the time Aoife and I went up to bed, they were usually picking at each other, slurring petty insults in sneering tones. Not long after, the shouting started.

On a good night, they stayed downstairs and threw barbed words and beer bottles at each other. On a bad night, my mom would come stumbling upstairs and drag Aoife and me out of bed, threatening to take us and leave Dad, screaming that she was going to sue him for divorce, and take the house and his family, and everyone was going to see what a loser he was. Just like his dad.

I remember cringing awake in the sudden glare as Mom snapped on the lights, and curling into a ball. I would squeeze my eyes shut and clench my jaw, praying for the lights to go off, and the darkness to come back. I was safe in the dark, with my pink stuffed pig cuddled to my chest and my big sister's back warm and solid against my own.

Aoife and I had our own beds, but we always slept together. She brought me into her bed for the first time when I was barely six months old. She'd heard me crying and had come into Mom and Dad's room to find me red-faced and screaming in the drawer Mom had rigged for me to sleep in, and Mom passed out across the bed. Aoife shook Mom, but she couldn't wake her up, no matter how hard she tried, and Dad was nowhere to be found.

Aoife wasn't quite four, but she remembered that night perfectly. Years later, she'd tell me the story of how she had made me a bottle of cold milk and then carried me into her bed. She said I stopped crying as soon as she fed me—even though the milk was cold—and that I'd snuggled against her ribs and slept the entire night through without a peep.

Growing up, I'd loved that story. It made me feel safe to know that my sister had always been there for me. Well, *safer*, anyway. As safe as I could feel considering the monsters under Aoife's and my shared bed were real. They were real and they lived at the end of the hall, and we never knew when they would tell us we were their beautiful little girls and cuddle us in their laps, and when they would take a switch to our bare legs for leaving our toys on the floor, or talking above a whisper.

My parents were changeable and terrifying, but the darkness was always the same. It was quiet and peaceful and hid me away in its gentle arms, rocking me to sleep.

I feel those arms around me now as I move through the tall grass behind Gabe's house. The darkness helps me hold myself together, keeping me safe, giving me strength. The Alexanders have cattle in the rear part of their back forty, but the pastures near Darby Hill are empty, and only harvested at the end of the summer for hay. Gabe told me once that Deborah couldn't stand to eat the beef that came from the cattle raised on the property if she had to look the cows in their big brown eyes every day.

Knowing what I do about Deborah, I find it hard to believe she would care that much about a *person*, let alone a cow, but people are strange. I once had a foster mother who brushed both of her Shih Tzu dogs for hours every day, attending to their grooming with a joy and tenderness that bordered on worship, while she let the children in her care go a week without a shower. Even her own two girls. Betty was crazy, but she couldn't be accused of treating her foster kids any worse than she treated her own children. She was fair and consistent in her neglect.

Fair and consistent.

I will be fair and consistent with my retribution. If Deborah and Aaron have lied to keep me from Gabe, I will treat them the same way Gabe and I treated the criminals Aaron worked so hard to keep out of prison. I will make them suffer, but only after I have Gabe safe in my arms.

I reach the edge of the field and climb lightly over the barbed wire fence, landing in a crouch on the other side, taking a moment to survey the plantation house. In the pale light of a sliver moon, Darby Hill is a hulking shadow, its silhouette barely visible against the black sky. Darkened windows reflect the faint moonlight, making them look like the eyes of a beast peering out from the trees surrounding the home. There isn't a light on anywhere that I can see, but it's after midnight and Gabe's parents go to bed early. One, or both, of them could be inside. I'll have to be careful until I make sure there is no one home to hear me rummaging around downstairs.

I pull my black sock mask down over my face, concealing everything but my eyes and mouth. Immediately, the familiar, job-in-progress energy casts its calming net over my thoughts. When I'm in my blacks, I'm reduced to the simplest version of myself. I become pure intention, driven by nothing but the determination to get in, get what I came for, and get out without getting caught.

It's strange to be in a situation like this without Gabe, but I have the soft leather gloves he gave me cradling my fingers, and the lock pick kit that was once his tucked into my back pocket. He is with me in spirit, and soon he will be with me in the flesh. I'm not leaving Darby Hill without the proof I came for, even if I have to go over every inch of the six thousand square foot home with a magnifying glass.

I move soundlessly down the stone pathway, through Deborah's lushly planted gardens, toward the servants' entrance. The door leads into the industrial-sized kitchen the late Grover Alexander added onto the home in the 1960's and is the easiest place to access the servants' staircase, the same staircase Gabe and I used to sneak upstairs before our second dinner with his parents.

We had crept up to his room and made love in his bed, hidden under his sinfully soft sheets, stealing one last blissful moment alone before sneaking back downstairs and running, laughing, around the side of the house to come in through the front door, greeting his parents as if we'd only just arrived.

The memory makes my chest ache as I squat in front of the door and pull out my tools, but I ignore the bittersweet longing pressing against my heart. This isn't the time to grieve, not when there's still a chance Gabe and I will have a chance to make new memories.

I slip the tension wrench into the keyhole and start to work, teasing the first pin into place. Thankfully, the lock is a fairly simple one, and after a few minutes of prodding at the remaining pins, the door handle gives under my hand with a soft click.

I step inside and close the door behind me,

turning to the alarm system's control panel on the wall to my right, and punching in the code. I shut the system down and turn to survey the darkened kitchen, noting the absence of cooking smells. On a normal night, the kitchen would still hold the lingering aromas of whatever gourmet meal Chef Jean-Luc had made the Alexanders for dinner. Rich, herb-and-wine-infused smells would fill the air, the scents of expensive foods prepared by a professional chef using only the finest ingredients. But tonight, there is only lemon-scented cleaner with the faint bitterness of coffee grounds lingering beneath.

It doesn't smell like a meal has been cooked here in days, and the house is so quiet it's hard to believe anyone but me is drawing breath inside it, but still, I start up the stairs instead of heading directly to the offices where I suspect I'll find what I've come for. I need to make sure Gabe's parents are gone—or at least sleeping—before I start poking around.

I pad up the wooden boards, staying close to the railing, remembering that the stairs squeak if you walk straight up the center. My heart beats faster, but I draw in slow, silent breaths. I have practice controlling my body's natural stress responses, but even that first night at the pawn-shop, I seemed to instinctively know how to keep my thoughts clear and my steps soft, how to ignore the anxiety pricking at my skin and focus on the job at hand. Gabe said it was like I was born to be a cat burglar.

I move past his room, peeking in only long enough to make sure the bed is empty before moving on. I can't go in there, no matter how much I want to climb into Gabe's bed and inhale the scent of him that might still be lingering on his sheets. There isn't time to waste indulging that soft, aching part of me. Tonight is about staying cold, calm, and focused on what I've come for.

By the time I reach the end of the long, wide, upstairs hallway, I've ducked into three guestrooms and the upstairs parlor, and found them all empty. The Alexanders' master bedroom is the last place I need to check, and the last room before the grand, central staircase that leads down to the front entryway.

I slow as I reach the half-open door, the hairs on my arms prickling beneath my long-sleeved black tee shirt. Until this moment, I've felt completely alone, but now the animal part of my brain warns that there is someone else nearby. I press my back against the wall, holding my breath as I lean in, peeking over my shoulder into the massive suite. I've only looked into this room once before, when Gabe's mother took me on a tour of the home, but I remember that the bed is on the far right of the room, flanked by two large, cherry armoires.

My eyes have already adjusted to the dim light of the hallway, so it only takes me a moment to make out the long shape under the covers on the far side of the bed. Judging by the size of the person, I'm pretty sure it's Gabe's father, and from the sound of his even breathing, it seems he's been asleep for a while. The other side of the bed is empty, the covers still spread up over the pillows.

It looks like he went to bed alone, which means Deborah might be somewhere downstairs…

Stomach churning with memories of that afternoon on the porch, when Deborah made it clear she held me responsible for her son's death, I ease past the doorway and start down the curved staircase leading to the ground floor. I cling to the side of the stairs nearest the wall, keeping as much of myself in the shadows as I can, straining to hear the sound of someone else moving around in the darkness.

I step off the last step onto the cold marble of the entryway with only the softest squeak of my boot against the smooth floor, but still I freeze. I hold completely still, ignoring the sweat prickling on my lip, and the slam-dancing of my heart against my ribs as I imagine Deborah rushing in from her office, phone in hand, ready to call the police.

I count silently to sixty, and only then do I start across the foyer. I check the large dining room, the study, and the library finding them all empty before ducking into Aaron's home office to find it equally deserted. I'm about to start back down the hall toward the front parlor and Deborah's office, when Aaron's computer emits a pinging sound. I can't imagine who would be emailing Mr. Alexander at one in the morning, and, after a moment, my curiosity gets the better of me.

I close the office door, sealing myself into the soft darkness. There are only two small windows in the office—both overlooking the garden behind the house—and it takes a moment for my eyes to adjust. When they do, I move around behind the desk, patting the area near the computer screen until I find the mouse and roll it back and forth.

The monitor crackles as it stirs to life. My eyelids twitch and my pupils contract as the blue glare becomes a bright white screen filled with several open word documents and a multi-tabbed Internet browser. Aaron's email inbox is in the open tab, showing one new message from Deborah Alexander.

My chest loosens at the site of Deborah's

name. It's doubtful that she'd be emailing her husband while they're both in the same house. Even before I click the message, I'm pretty certain Deborah is out of town, but the first line of her email confirms it.

I can't believe you left me. I don't care how long you've been waiting for this hearing. You should be here. I can't do this alone. I can't sleep and I can't eat and I can't stop thinking...

The weight of this is...too much. I need to talk.

If you're awake, call. I won't be sleeping anytime soon.

I scan the email three times, my heart beating faster with each repeated reading. Deborah must be with Gabe. She must be! And things must not be going the way she hoped they would. Why else would she sound so upset? If Gabe were dead, there would be no need for her to be stressed out and sleepless. If Gabe were dead, there would be nothing left to talk about.

I'm getting ready to search the rest of Mr. Alexander's emails—certain I'm on my way to figuring out where his parents have taken Gabe—when the message updates, indicating a response from Gabe's dad.

My hand turns to stone on the mouse, and my stomach drops.

Gabe's dad is awake. He's awake upstairs, and apparently checking his email. Now, I just have to pray he doesn't decide to come down to his office. If he does, I'll be trapped. There's only one way out, and the chances that I'll make it past Mr. Alexander, through the library, into the dining room, and out the bay doors leading to the garden without getting caught are slim. I'm fast, but Gabe's dad is in incredible shape for an older man, and has ten inches and at least a hundred pounds on me.

I hold my breath, hand shaking as I click the email, needing to know how Gabe's father replied to his wife more than I need to ensure my own safety.

I'm sorry. I know this is an incredibly hard time. Try to get some rest. I put the ashes in your office, and I've contacted Charlene. She's taking care of the rest of it.

I'll call you first thing in the morning before I go into court.

Love you.

Ashes.

The word is a bomb ripping through what's left of my heart.

CHAPTER THIRTEEN

CAITLIN

"And if God choose, I shall
but love thee better after death."
-Elizabeth Barrett Browning

*a*shes.

I shake my head, not wanting to make sense of the word.

Ashes. Rising from the ashes. Smoke and ashes. Ashes to ashes...

Maybe Gabe hasn't been buried because...

Because...

Ashes to ashes. Dust to dust.

My hand slips from the mouse. I stand, feeling each link in my spine slide into place as I straighten. I'm acutely aware of the way my muscles flex and release to move my feet across the thick carpet, of my heart beating and my blood rushing, of my breath feathering over my too warm lips.

I move through the library and into the hall, feeling strangely ethereal, light and airy, like a ghost haunting the dark belly of Darby Hill. I'm only half in my body, watching myself from a distance as I make the turn into the front parlor and move on into Deborah's office.

There's a light on inside. In the corner of the room, a green lamp with a pink bulb casts the surface of her desk in a rosy glow. There is a small silver laptop on the right side of the desk, a stack of personal stationary and an antique fountain pen in the center, and on the left hand side, an urn. It is also silver, but duller, brushed silver as expensive looking as the heavy Rolex watch Gabe wore on Sundays.

He would wear the watch to church with his parents, and then forget to take it off after. I remember watching the heavy band slip around his wrist as he ate his burger at our weekly family burger night, thinking how sexy it looked against his tan skin. One night, right after I'd bitten into his muscled forearm just above the watch, I told him how much I liked him in a little jewelry.

Gabe had laughed, and promised to invest in more masculine decoration, like a thick gold chain to hang around his neck that spelled out his name. I'd suggested "Property of Caitlin Cooney," instead, but Gabe had dismissed that as being too long. He'd said he'd shorten it to "CC's" and have the apostrophe formed from jade the same color as my eyes. I'd laughed at the joke, but I'd been touched, too. I loved that he was mine, and knew that he'd have the ridiculous necklace made and wear it just for me if I'd asked him to.

But now…

Now…

I pick up the urn. It is heavy. I remove the lid with one trembling hand. It is full, almost to the top. The ash is fine and gray and smells very faintly of metal. It does not smell of Gabe, of secrets and spice and long summer nights and the best kind of trouble. It does not smell of the place where his neck met his shoulder or his breath after he kissed me every place he could think to kiss me. It doesn't smell like safety and love and danger and happiness and home. It does not smell alive.

Gabe isn't alive. Gabe is here in this urn, burned to ash, all the unpredictable, passionate pieces of the man I loved reduced to a few pounds of gray powder. Despair floods through me, a molten sadness so hot it feels like I'm going to catch fire and burn to ash myself, but I don't.

And I don't cry.

I put the lid on the urn and set it back on the desk. Then I turn and walk back through the lonely halls of Darby Hill. I don't bother trying to be quiet, but I don't make much noise. I don't think I could, even if I tried. I'm too hollow to disturb the silence in this house, this world, a world without Gabe.

He's gone. He's really gone and now there is no hope. I feel it leak away, leaving me heavier than I was before. I am a stone sinking to the bottom of an ice-cold winter river, never to rise again.

I arm the security system and let myself out the servants' entrance door. I close it behind me and walk through the garden, not feeling the uneven stones beneath my feet. I climb over the fence into the pasture and aim my body toward where I parked the van on a narrow gravel road two miles from Darby Hill, but somewhere between the pasture, the stretch of forested land on the other side, and the van, I lose time.

I leave my body, but I don't know where I go. I don't remember what I was thinking, or when I decided to keep walking and walking, far past the place where I parked, so far down a narrow country road headed east that I'm nearly at the county line by the time I come back to myself.

I slip into my skin as the sun is rising, painting the sky behind the rolling hills a giddy shade of pink. I become suddenly, acutely aware of pain in my legs and hips, and a cramping sensation in my right calf. I shuffle to a stop, my shoes scattering gravel along the shoulder of the unfamiliar road. I pull in a deep breath and let it out, my sigh carried away by a cool morning breeze that sweeps across my face.

My mask is gone, but I don't remember what I did with it. My gloves are gone, too, and I've stripped off my long-sleeved shirt, leaving me in nothing but my favorite green tank top. I'm not wearing a bra, something that usually wouldn't bother me, but this morning my breasts feel sore and achy. The sensation makes me suspect that I might have been running at some point, but I don't remember.

I don't want to remember anything about last night, but I do. I may have lost time between the plantation and wherever I am now, but I remember everything that happened inside Darby Hill. I remember and I hurt, but I still don't cry. I simply stand there on the side of the road and watch the pink sky blush and burn and the sun come peeking over the mountains like a promise.

There is still light, it says. There is still something to live for.

"Danny, Ray, Sean, and Emmie," I whisper softly to the sun, their names like a prayer, a rope pulling me from the depths. "Danny, Ray, Sean, and Emmie. Danny, Ray, Sean, and Emmie and..."

My hands come to my abdomen, hovering over the flat place between my hip bones, that almost concave expanse that seems too narrow and empty to contain life, but I suddenly know it is not. At that moment, staring into the sun in the middle of nowhere, I know I am pregnant. I know it the way I know winter nights are long and summer days even longer. I feel it in every thump of my heart, every soft whoosh of blood flowing beneath my skin. I know I'm going to have a baby, and if it is a boy, I will name him Gabriel.

"Gabe." The sound of his name floating away in the crisp morning air breaks the dam. I finally cry, but I don't sob. My violent, rage-filled grief passed days ago. These are different tears, silent, hopeless tears that streak down my cheeks in lazy rivulets.

I stand staring into the sunrise, crying until the sun crests the top of the mountains and begins to beat down upon my face. Within moments, the air heats up, becoming thick and muggy, making it harder to draw in a deep breath. Soon, it will be another scorcher, another day to spend inside the house hiding from the miserable heat and humidity of a South Carolina summer.

The thought of going home and shutting myself back inside the house is unfathomable. I don't want to be there anymore. I don't want to sleep in my bed where the ghost of Gabe's touch haunts me. I don't want to take a bath in the bathtub where he washed my hair, and promised me he'd love me until men are fairy tales and the world catches fire. I can't. I can't face those daily reminders without falling apart. I need a fresh start. We all do. Me, my brothers, Emmie...and the baby who is on his way to us.

Decision made, I reach for my back pocket, grateful to feel the slim, hard rectangle of my cell still shoved deep inside. I'm not sure where my shirt, my gloves, or my mask are, but I still have my cell and the keys to the van.

I also have ten missed calls from Sherry, and a few from the landline at the house.

The first call I place is to Sherry, who answers on the first ring. I assure her I'm fine, and tell her the name of the road I'm on, and that I think I'm nearly in York County. She tells me to hang tight and promises to pick me up in twenty minutes. She doesn't yell at me for not answering the phone all night, or ask how I ended up in the middle of nowhere. Most importantly, she doesn't ask what I found out about Gabe. Sherry's been my best friend since we were little. She knows me well enough to hear the despair in my voice, and to understand no news from me never means good news.

I end the call—grateful for Sherry, and for being spared having to explain—and place another call. My dad doesn't answer on the first ring. He answers on the fifth, with a grunt, and a slurred hello that makes it obvious he was still asleep.

"I want the house in Hawaii," I say, not bothering to tell him it's me or to apologize for waking him up with the sunrise. "How soon can we make it happen?"

"Great, great," Chuck mumbles, followed by a long yawn. "Smart decision, Kit Cat. I thought you would come around. You're too smart to pass up an opportunity like this."

"How soon, Dad?" I repeat, hating the happiness in his sleepy voice. "I want to get the kids moved and settled in before school starts."

Chuck sniffs and clears his throat. "Um...I don't know. I'll have to check. Check with the lawyers. They should know. I'll call them as soon as I get the crust from my eyeballs, and grab a shower."

I hear a woman's voice mumbling in the background, clearly irritated.

"After I get a shower and run to the store for Veronica," Chuck amends. "We're out of coffee and half-and-half. Can't call lawyers before coffee."

"Fine," I say, knowing pushing him won't get me an answer any faster. "But let me know as soon as you know, okay? And I want us to file the paperwork for custody of the kids later today. I have everything ready. We both just need to sign, and take the paperwork to the courthouse."

"Sounds good," Chuck says in a positively upbeat voice, making it hard to believe he was so set on fighting my bid for custody just a week ago. But I never bought that he cared about being a legal parent to the kids. He just didn't want to lose part of his check, or transfer ownership of the house.

"So I'm assuming you'll want to keep your whole check, as well as the house in Giffney?" I ask, needing to confirm my suspicion.

"Well, you and the boys will have that nice rental property," Chuck says. "That's three times what you were going to get from me. Doesn't seem like you'll need—"

"Fine," I say, cutting him off. "Assuming everything in Hawaii checks out, we won't need your check. But I want to talk to the lawyers myself. Text me their name and number as soon as you get the chance."

"Aye aye, Captain," Chuck says.

I end the call without a good-bye. I can't stand to listen to his chipper bullshit anymore.

I'll get the names of the lawyers, have Sherry work her Google-Fu to make sure everything in Hawaii is legit, and then it won't matter if Chuck thinks he's pulled one over on me. As long as the kids have a home—a home far away from Giffney, all our family's baggage, and all this summer's horrible memories—I don't care what's going on in Chuck's twisted little mind.

I stuff the phone into my back pocket and turn my back to the sun, letting it burn the bare skin of my neck. Working indoors as much as I do, I haven't had a tan in years. I wonder what it will be like to have time to get out during the day, to take the kids to the beach, to raise Gabe's and my child in an entirely different world from the narrow-minded small town where I grew up.

Our child. My hands come to my abdomen again, and I swear I can feel the presence of a tiny spark, the surge of a brand new heart beating inside of me. That surety is the only thing that keeps me from bursting into tears when Sherry pulls up beside me, and opens the passenger's door to her VW bug. Without this part of Gabe to cling to, I wouldn't be able to handle the pity in her eyes.

"Do you want to talk about it?" she asks as I slide into the passenger's seat.

I shake my head. "I want to go home. Start packing."

Sherry's eyebrows lift as she turns the car around to head back toward town. "Where are you going?"

"Me and the kids are moving to Hawaii."

Sherry slams on the breaks in the middle of the narrow road, making my seatbelt lock tight across my chest. "What?"

"Dad inherited a house there," I say, tightening my sagging ponytail. "He said he'll give it to me in exchange for letting him keep the house here. Assuming it checks out, we're moving. Soon. I can't be here anymore."

Sherry blinks like she's trying to wake up from a long nap, drawing my attention to the blue smudges beneath her eyes. It doesn't look like she slept well last night, which is my fault, no doubt. I told her I'd be home no later than two, and instead I was gone all night and didn't answer any of her calls.

"I'm sorry for worrying you," I say. "I didn't feel the phone vibrate."

She reaches out, covering my hand with hers. "Don't worry about it, babe. I'm just glad you're okay, but I…"

I lift my eyebrows, knowing that's all the encouragement Sherry needs to keep talking.

"I'm going to miss you," she says with a self-conscious shrug. "I know it's selfish of me, but I don't like the thought of this town without my best friend in it."

"Then…come with us," I say, on impulse.

Sherry snorts as she rolls her eyes. "Yeah right."

"No, seriously. Come. You and I can share a room," I say, liking the idea more every minute. I don't like the idea of leaving her behind, either, especially since I just lost my other best friend.

Isaac still brings pizza over for the kids and calls to check up on me, but things haven't been the same since the night he confessed he wanted more than friendship, and I told him I would never see him that way. My heart belongs to Gabe, he was my first, my last, and my only, and that's how it's going to stay.

"I can't move to Hawaii," Sherry says, wrinkling her nose.

"Why not?" I roll down the window, letting in a too-warm breeze.

"What about my job at the flower shop?"

"They have flower shops in Hawaii, and Carla would give you a great reference."

"What about my sister and Bill?" Sherry protests, but I can see the excitement creeping into her bright amber eyes. "They say they're going to try for a baby soon, and need me to help out."

"If or when that happens, you can move back," I say, not wanting to say anything about another baby who might need her, not until I have a test in my hand to prove that the child I'm carrying isn't wishful thinking.

Sherry shakes her head so hard her curls seem to grow an inch longer. "This is crazy. You don't want to share a room with me. I'm messy and loud, and what if you decide you want privacy? Like guy and girl type privacy?"

I wince at the thought of any man but Gabe touching me, and Sherry squeezes my arm.

"I'm so sorry," she whispers. "I know that's not where your head is, at all. I'm just tired, and when I'm tired I run my mouth without thinking. It's like verbal diarrhea."

"It's okay," I say, patting the back of her hand. "Just say you'll come. I really want you to. I'll even pay for your ticket."

Sherry shakes her head again. "I've got enough to pay my own way. I've saved a ton living with my sister for two years." She pauses, pulling in a breath as her fingers slip from my arm. "I guess I'm really thinking about this."

"I'd say you're more than thinking about it."

"You're right," she says, a smile teasing at her lips before her expression grows serious once more. "But I wish this adventure was happening for different reasons."

I nod and cast my eyes down to the floor mat, remembering the night I sat in the driver seat of Sherry's car and Gabe sat next to me, teasing me, challenging me, asking me hard questions and refusing to settle for easy answers. I fell for him that first night, and I'll never forget him, but leaving Giffney is for the best. He's everywhere here, even in my best friend's car. Memories of him might one day be the balm that heals all the broken things inside of me, but right now they're just tearing me apart.

Sherry and I are quiet on the drive back to where I parked the van. She turns on the country station, but she doesn't hum along the way she usually would. Maybe she's thinking about Gabe, or about the fresh start waiting for us on an island far away. I don't know, and I don't ask. I'm too busy promising myself I will be strong for the kids, for the memory of Gabe, and thinking about a little boy or girl with Gabe's dark hair and bright blue eyes.

CHAPTER FOURTEEN

CAITLIN

"Touch it: the marble eyes are not wet
If it could weep, it could arise and go."
-Elizabeth Barrett Browning

It takes three weeks and more paperwork than I've signed in my entire life, but finally the house in Hawaii is in my name, custody of the kids is finalized, the plane tickets are purchased, the kids' clothes and toys are packed—I allow them one suitcase each, warding off whining with a promise to buy everyone a "welcome to Hawaii" toy or videogame as soon as we're settled—and we're on our way to the airport in Charleston.

Chuck drives all the Cooneys in the family

van. Sherry will be delivered by her sister, since there wasn't room for Sherry *and* her three suitcases in the van. Sherry's taking more luggage than Danny and me combined, but I don't care. I've seen pictures of the house in Maui. The loft room Sherry and I will share is enormous, big enough for a king-sized bed, three chests of drawers, a home office in one corner, and a loveseat and overstuffed chair pulled up in front of the ocean-facing windows. There will be more than enough room for her stuff, my stuff, and, when the time comes, a crib and changing table.

I took the test two weeks ago. I was only a day late, but the two lines popped up right away, bright and pink, like I'd known they would. I called an OB/GYN in Maui that afternoon, and scheduled my first prenatal appointment for two weeks after we land.

I haven't told Sherry or the boys yet. I want to warm myself with the secret a little longer. It makes me feel closer to Gabe, being the only one who knows about our baby, the son or daughter who will be born on an island in the sun and never know what it feels like for a snowflake to melt on his or her face.

We're never coming back to Giffney. I told Chuck he'd have to come to us if he wants to see the kids, and even he agreed a clean break was for the best. He told me to go and grab at my new life with both hands, and he'd come to visit when he could. He probably won't, but that's okay. After the past few weeks of generosity and cooperation, I'm feeling closer to Chuck than I have in a long time, but not so close I'm going to mourn the loss of an unpredictable alcoholic in my life. Our past is too long and twisted to be smoothed out so easily. Our relationship has left calloused places on my heart that make it impossible for me to feel anything too deeply where he is concerned.

Not that I've been feeling much lately, anyway. Since the night I found Gabe's ashes, I've only rarely been completely present in my body. It's as if my soul is keeping its distance from my skin and bones, realizing it might do damage if it gets too close. I'm not finished mourning Gabe, not by a long shot, but right now protecting the health of our baby is the most important thing. I can't indulge the heart shattering grief that's hovering in the wings, waiting for a chance to sweep in and take center stage and destroy any chance of remaining functional. I must continue to function, and eventually thrive, for my son or daughter and the rest of the kids, if not for myself.

"Well, here we are." Chuck pulls up to the curb at the airport, a grin on his face so wide you'd think he was the one moving to Maui. But then,

Veronica is pretty damned excited about moving into a bigger house, even if it is a dump like ours. Tonight, she'll probably make Chuck an extra spicy batch of her famous meatballs, they'll have ten or twelve beers each, and Chuck will feel like a king in his castle.

Everybody wins. Everybody except me and Gabe, who were doomed before we even got started.

"That's the last of it," Chuck says, heaving the final suitcase up onto the curb, where Danny grabs it and loads it onto the luggage cart.

"Thanks for everything, Dad." I unbuckle Emmie and scoop her out of her car seat, balancing her on my hip as I lean in to hug Chuck goodbye.

"Take care, Caity Did." Chuck kisses my cheek, then Emmie's. "Hope the island life treats you right."

I watch as Chuck hugs Ray and Sean, then settles for a handshake from Danny, who is still suspicious of the move and swears we're going to land in Hawaii and find out the house is a scam, no matter how many times I've assured him that the lawyers are legit and I've triple-checked all the paperwork.

But I understand why Danny's holding back on believing in our family's good fortune. There's nothing more painful than believing in something you want so badly, and then having it ripped away. It's like pouring acid into a wound you thought had healed, a hundred times worse than if you'd never let yourself believe in the first place. Danny's simply protecting himself, refusing to let hope in until it's standing on the step, pounding at the door.

I'm the same way. I've made all the plans, but I won't believe it's going to work out until I sleep my first night in the house in Hawaii without it crumbling down around me. I learned my lesson about believing in the impossible that night in Deborah's office, when I held Gabe's ashes in my hands. The invitation to his funeral—and the letter from Gabe's father suggesting it might be best if I didn't come—came the next day.

"Can you walk for me, doodle?" I ask Emmie as we start into the terminal to wait for Sherry before we get in line for security.

"Yes," Emmie says, taking my hand as I set her on her feet. "I big."

"You are big," I agree, though Emmie's small for a nearly-three-year-old.

Still, I'm not sure I should be carrying anything over twenty pounds while I'm pregnant. It's better that Emmie gets used to not being carried as much. We can get our snuggle time in while we're sitting down. In fact, I'm counting on it. On bad days, when missing Gabe is like a knife shoved into my heart, Emmie snuggles are the only things that get me through.

Danny leads the way through the ticketing area, pushing our overloaded luggage cart with an ease and confidence that makes me aware of how much he's grown. Ray and Sean follow not far behind, arguing about a video game they've been trying to beat and shoving each other every few steps, but I don't yell at them. I've been so tired lately that I save my yelling for Code Red misbehavior.

"Sherry!" Emmie jumps up and down, tugging at my arm as she points toward the women's restroom, where a tall redhead with curls almost as kinky as Sherry's is bent over getting a drink.

"No, not Sherry," I say. "But she'll be here soon. Let's go find some breakfast, and I'll text her to see how far away she is."

"Sherry!" Emmie insists, a whine creeping into her voice, making me hope she'll be able to nap on the plane. I had to get her out of bed at five a.m. to get her ready to go, and Emmie isn't her usual sweet, easy-going self without a solid twelve hours of sleep.

"That's not Sherry, sweetie," I repeat, digging into my purse with one hand, searching for my phone. "But we can call her in just a sec."

I paw through my purse, but no matter which

pocket I wiggle my hand into, I can't find my phone.

"Hey, Danny, wait up," I call out. "I can't find my phone. I want to make sure I didn't leave it in the van before Chuck gets too far away."

Danny stops the cart and leans against our mountain of luggage with an eye roll that makes it obvious how frustrating I am, and reminds me that my oldest brother isn't much better than a three-year-old when he's sleep deprived. I drop Emmie's hand and use both hands to dig through my purse. I finally find the phone buried beneath my wallet and pull it out with a relieved sigh. "Okay, I've got it. We're good."

Danny starts pushing the cart toward security again, and I reclaim Emmie's hand before tapping Sherry's name on my phone. It rings twice before she picks up.

"Sorry!" she says, before I can get a word in. "The truck was almost out of gas when we left the house. We had to stop at the Mobile near the highway. I'll be there in ten minutes."

"No worries," I say, glancing down at Emmie, who is tugging on my arm again. "We're going to-
--"

"Gabe!" Emmie says, pointing back behind us, sending a shockwave of misery zinging through my chest. This isn't the first time she's said his name since he died, but it's the first time she's

mistaken someone else for Gabe. She does this a
lot—she seems to have a hard time telling grown-
ups apart—but for some reason it hits me hard
this morning, making my throat so tight I can't
answer the first time Sherry says my name.

"Caitlin?" she says again. "Are you still there?"

"Ye-yes," I stammer, tightening my grip on
Emmie's hand when she repeats Gabe's name and
tries to pull away. "Just having a little trouble
wrangling the savages on my own. We had to get
up early to get going, and everyone's cranky."

"I'll be there to help wrangle any minute,"
Sherry says. "Hang in there, soldier."

"Will do. See you soon." I end the call, shove
my phone into my purse, and reach down,
scooping Emmie into my arms. I kiss her cheek,
ignoring the fussy sound she makes, and blow a
raspberry on her neck. Her whine transforms to
a high-pitched giggle that makes it impossible
not to smile.

"Gotcha," I say, laughing as I press another
kiss to her forehead. She pats my cheeks with her
warm, sticky hands and I smile again. There is
pain and grief, but there is this, too.

There is still love in the world, and from now
on I will never take a single moment of it for
granted.

CHAPTER FIFTEEN

GABE

"'Tis in...memory...."

I watch the little girl with the blond curls pat her young mother's cheeks, then kiss her nose. The mother laughs, the smile on her face so warm and full of love seeing it makes my heart feel like it's going to rip free from my chest.

For the first time since the surgery, I experience a pain worse than the pain in my head. For the first time in weeks, the fog that has clouded my every thought lifts and I experience a moment of clarity—sharp and brutal, like a knife slipped between my ribs.

I *want* that. I want to treasure someone that

much. I want someone to look at me the way that mother and daughter are looking at each other. They are both so beautiful, feeling so much, holding nothing back. It's painful to watch them embrace, the little girl hugging her mom's neck so tight, the mom kissing her daughter's curls with a tenderness that makes it clear they are everything to each other. They're too far away for me to hear what they're saying, but I imagine that it's something sweet.

"Are you ready to go, Gabe?" Olia, my private nurse, returns from the bathroom, taking her position at the back of my wheelchair.

I shake my head. "One...minute."

I don't want to go yet. I want the little girl to look at me again. I want her mother to turn my way and see me, even if I am a wasted, faded version of myself. Even if I am in this chair with a nurse escorting me home, a woman who, until a week ago, had to help me wipe my ass. Olia still has to help me onto the toilet, and pull up my pants when I'm finished like I'm no bigger than the toddler in the young woman's arms.

I know I'm no prize, and that the woman is probably married, anyway, but I still want the blonde to look at me. I want to see her eyes. Somehow, I know they will be green. They will be the pale green of that milky green stone...

What's the name? The one they used to carve figurines and chess pieces a long time ago...

I curse beneath my breath and give up searching for the missing word. I can't remember the damned stone's name.

There are so many things I can't remember, words and phrases and months of my life lost along with the tumor they whittled free. The surgeon said I might never see those memories again, but Bea, the nurse who watched over me before Olia, promised there was hope.

In the early days, when no one was sure if I would pull through, Bea would talk to me while she changed my various tubes and checked my beeping machines. She said that brain surgery is like an earthquake. It shakes things loose, transforming the landscape of the mind, but not destroying as much as it might seem at first. The missing pieces are still there, buried beneath the rubble, or exiled on the other side of the chasm surgery leaves behind. She said there could come a day when I'd find a way to those memories, and reclaim the things that I've lost.

But it will take time. At least a year. Maybe more. Endless days I will spend lost in a fog of pain, struggling to reconcile who my parents insist I was before the surgery with who I am now.

Sometimes, listening to them talk, I think the

doctor may have cut away more of me than Aaron and Deborah can imagine. I don't feel like the happy, well-adjusted, driven pre-law major they insist I was before. There is darkness inside of me, a rage and sadness that is bigger than post-surgical depression. Sometimes I get so angry it frightens me.

The things I want to do, the things I imagine...

They aren't pretty. They aren't sane or healthy, and, until this morning, I was beginning to think that my soul was a broken, twisted thing. Whether the surgery was to blame, or I was always a monster hiding behind a handsome face, I didn't know. I only knew that I was full of hate and misery and there was no room for anything else. I felt no gratitude to the doctor who saved my life against all odds; I felt no affection for my parents. I haven't even been happy to be alive, because what good is life without something to live for, something other than this emptiness that has threatened to swallow me whole?

But now, looking at this woman, this girl—she can't be much older than I am, even if she is a mother—I feel something. There is a softening inside me, a bruised place on my heart that makes my ribs ache and my throat tight. A wave of longing sweeps through me, making me shake with the force of how much I want.

I want to love someone. I *need* to love some-one. I need to love someone the way I loved...

I close my eyes, chest lurching as a ghost of a memory dances through my head. It's a wispy, transparent memory, with graceful arms, a wicked smile, and perfect, moon-shaped toes. I see chipped nail polish and bare feet against concrete steps. I hear a throaty laugh in the dark-ness and feel hot breath on my lips as arms pull me down onto a lumpy bed. My head spins with the sense memories of nails digging into my shoulders, the tang of sweet, salty sweat in my mouth.

For a moment the pieces of the mystery struggle to come together, but then they're gone. The memory slips through my fingers, turning to smoke in my hands.

By the time I open my eyes, the beautiful woman and her daughter are walking away, moving toward the security line, a redheaded woman now by their side. I watch them go with a ridiculous sense of loss, hating myself for not calling out, even if the blonde is a stranger. I should have said something. I should have told her thank you for giving me hope that I am more than a monster, that there may still be good left inside of me.

But I didn't, and the moment is gone.

Now, it's time for Olia to push me outside to

the curb, where my mother is waiting in the new van, the one specially equipped to fit my chair. The doctors don't know how long it will be before I recover the ability to walk. It could be weeks, months, years.

Or never. Some people never rebuild the bridges their tumors ate away. Some people stay lost in the wilderness without ever finding their way home.

Home. Staring at the blonde's retreating form, I realize it isn't a place. It is a touch, a gentle word, a tender look. It is knowing that there is someone out there who knows all your secrets, has looked into all your dark corners, and loves you anyway. It is realizing that you are not alone.

I am not alone. Someone—that ghost with the moon-shaped toes—loved me, once. And I loved her, with all the ferocity I've done my best to keep hidden from my parents since the moment I opened my eyes after the surgery. I loved a girl who cherished my rough edges and dark corners, who took me as I am, who kissed me in the shadows and taught me that even the most jagged puzzle pieces have a place where they will fit. Just right. Flush and snug and suddenly whole.

I can't remember her name, or her face. I can't remember when we met, or how long we loved, or why she isn't here with me now, but the fact that she existed is enough to steady my hands and calm my racing heart. I found her once. I can find her again. I can search for her in the jungles of my mind until I find a clue, a trail of bread-crumbs, something that will lead me back to what I've lost.

Back to her.

CHAPTER SIXTEEN

CAITLIN

One Year Later...

"The face of all the word is changed, I think,
Since I first heard the footsteps of they soul.
Move still, oh, still, beside me."
-Elizabeth Barrett Browning

$\mathcal{I}$'m falling again.

I'm always falling.

In my dreams, I've taken that one wrong step a hundred thousand times, my subconscious mind struggling to go back to the moment I lost my last link to Gabe and rewrite history.

But even my dreams turn against me. Sometimes I make it down the stairs to the loft, only to trip on the stone path outside the front door to the cottage, and go tumbling down the hill. Sometimes I make it down the hill and into the car, only for the tires to skid on the rain-slick streets and send the car hurtling through the guardrail, into the sea.

Sometimes, I'm back in Pitt's attic, strangling the life out of him, and the moment he dies, the cramps hit, ripping through my core, taking a life for a life, every wave of pain assuring me that monsters don't live happily ever after. Murderers don't get to have a baby with ten perfect fingers and toes. Murderers get pain and misery and blood for blood.

No matter how the dream plays out, the end is always the same. I am always on my back staring up at the ceiling or the sky, with pain rocketing up and down my spine, agony fisting around my abdomen, and horrible, wet heat flowing between my legs. I always lose the baby. Every single time.

I wake up from the dreams with tears on my cheeks and my heart aching like it's going to explode and a scream pushing at my lips, struggling to fight free of my mouth. But I never let the scream out. If I do, I know I might have trouble stopping.

Tonight, I sit up in bed, trembling in the darkness, listening to the island wind whip the palm trees outside my window. I swipe the tears from my cheeks, and take deep, silent breaths, fighting to get myself under control before I wake up Isaac. But I should know better. Most of the time, Isaac sleeps like a rock, but it's like he can sense it when I'm really upset, even when he's unconscious. He calls it his Caitlin-dar, and it is almost always dead on.

"Bad dream?" he asks, his voice a sleepy rumble as he reaches out, running one big hand up and down my spine through my thin sleep shirt. The trade winds keep the lower floor, where the kids sleep, cool, but it's warmer up here in the loft. Warm enough that Isaac sleeps in nothing but his boxers, and I in a tee shirt and panties.

"Yeah." I take another shuddery breath. "It's okay. I'll be fine."

I don't tell him that I'm starting to think I *won't* be fine, that I'll never stop reliving losing Gabe, then losing our baby four months into the pregnancy. I don't tell Isaac that I'm afraid I'll never feel whole again, or that no amount of happiness or love or understanding will ever make up for the things I've lost.

I don't want Isaac to know. After all he's done for me and the kids, I don't want him to realize that one half of the life we're making together is built on a lie, and that I've only been pretending to get back to normal. In truth, I'm not sure I know what normal is anymore. Most of the past year has felt like a dream, a mix of nightmares and wishes come true that have left me feeling permanently off-kilter.

The day after I lost the baby—a little boy so tiny he never had a chance of living outside my body once my water broke—Isaac flew to the island. He sat by my hospital bed and coaxed food and water between my lips. He carried me to the car and then up to my bedroom at the cottage. He called his parents, said he wasn't coming home, and got a job at the local flatbread company making pizzas until he could find something better. He shifted his entire life around to help Sherry take care of the kids during the month it took for me to emerge from my haze of despair and grief, and never once complained.

And when I was finally up and doing better—going through the motions, if not living the way I had before—he rented a room in a house of Australian surfers down the street and stayed on the island. He did it to be close to me and the kids, to be the kind of friend he's always been, the kind who loves with his entire heart. It took a few months, but by the time the winter rains battered the roof of our cozy new home, Sherry had moved in with her new boyfriend in the next village over, and Isaac was sleeping over at our house once or twice a week.

At first, all we did was hold each other. He would pull my back against his front and curl his big, warm body around me, and I would feel safe for the first time in longer than I could remember. Eventually, cuddling turned to kissing, and then to painfully gentle lovemaking so different than what I had with Gabe, but sweet, and good. I can feel how much Isaac loves me in every kiss, every caress, and I can hardly fault him for treating me like I might break if he kisses me too hard.

Since I lost the baby, I haven't been as strong as I used to be. I enrolled in college and am working on getting my degree in social work. I've been taking care of the kids, making new friends, and spending time with Sherry, but I have done it all while walking on eggshells, as if I'm balancing on a razor's edge and this new life could come crumbling down around me at any moment. I have been distant, colder, too careful, and so much less than Isaac or the kids deserve.

I want to change. I want to lock the past away and only visit it when I choose to page through those beautiful, painful memories, but so far I haven't been able to. I am a shadow, and I don't know how to firm myself back up again.

"Same dream?" Isaac asks, still rubbing my back, though now he makes slow circles between my hunched shoulders. I nod, but don't say a word. I don't want to talk about it. Talking never helps, but sometimes touching does.

I push the covers down to the foot of the bed before I turn and straddle Isaac's hips, not surprised to find him hard, his cock straining the front of his boxers. I tease him that he has a perpetual hard-on; he insists there are much worse problems, and I agree. There are much worse problems, and I like the fact that he's always ready, always hot and hard and eager to give me the oblivion I crave.

"Off." I curl my fingers around the waistband of his boxers and tug.

"Yes ma'am." He lifts his hips and I drag his underwear down his thick, furry legs and toss the boxers to the floor before straddling him again. I lean down, capturing his lips for a kiss as I roll my hips, sighing as his bare cock rubs against me through my panties.

"God, you feel good," he mumbles against my lips as his big hands move beneath my tee shirt, smoothing up my ribs to capture my breasts, one in each wide palm.

He teases my nipples into tight points, sending waves of desire crashing between my legs, dampening the crotch of my panties. I moan into his mouth and increase my rhythm, grinding faster, harder against him, until he grunts and his hands drop to my hips stilling me with a gentle squeeze.

"Not so rough, tiger," he says, hooking his thumbs into the sides of my panties and tugging them down.

I straighten my legs and curve my body to one side, helping him dispose of my underwear, trying to ignore the disappointment that flashes through my chest. I remind myself to make an effort to be the kind of lover Isaac wants me to be, but when I spread my legs again, sliding my slick center up and down his bare cock, I'm not as gentle as I know he would prefer.

I don't want gentle tonight. I want to bruise him with my want. I want him to spread me wide and drive inside me until I cry out. I want him to fuck me hard, not like I'm made of glass, but like I am strong and wild and his equal in every way. Isaac has over a foot on me in height, but I could handle anything he could dish out. I crave the feel of him pounding into my core, taking me hard, banishing my awareness of everything but how good it feels to come together without either of us holding back.

But when Isaac's hands circle my waist and he shifts my hips, he positions his cock at my entrance and lowers me with infinite care. He pushes into me, inch by careful inch, so slow and easy my body has plenty of time to accommodate him and it doesn't hurt at all, even when he reaches the end of me and we have to shift back and forth until we find the angle that lets me accept his entire length.

Despite the difference in our heights, Gabe and I fit perfectly together, no matter what position we chose, but with Isaac, it's difficult. Only one angle works, and in any position but one, I am smothered by his chest, or in need of dozens of pillows to prop up my knees. And so, I am on top.

I'm always on top, but I'm not calling the shots.

Isaac takes the lead when we're in bed together, in a big-brotherly sort of way. He watches out for me, takes care of me, and makes sure I don't get hurt, but he isn't controlling my pleasure. He isn't demanding I spread my body and finger myself while he watches; he doesn't warn me not to come until he says I can, or he'll punish me in a thousand wonderfully wicked ways. For all his immense size and strength, Isaac isn't a dominant partner. He's a gentle giant, a caregiver who doesn't seem to mind that when lovemaking is this careful it takes at least twenty minutes, and endless teasing of my nipples with his fingers and tongue, to get me off.

He is patient and determined, and when I finally come—throwing back my head, squeezing my eyes shut, and trying my best not to see any face but Isaac's in the darkness behind my lids— the sound he makes is pure satisfaction. Even before he comes, his cock jerking languidly inside of me, even his orgasm a hundred shades less violent than Gabe's, he sounds fulfilled. My pleasure is his pleasure, the way it should be between a man and a woman, the way it was between me and Gabe.

I sag forward onto Isaac's chest, catching my breath, wishing I felt the same way he feels. I wish I could love him the way he deserves to be loved. I wish he could be everything to me, but no matter how hard I try, the love I feel for him remains a warm, complacent thing.

This love doesn't burn inside of me, threatening to consume me even as it builds me up, making me something stronger and better than I was before. This love doesn't reach down deep and awaken the wild side of me, that part that will fight to the death to protect the things it holds dear, that part that is both beautiful and vicious, as terrifying as it is intoxicating. This love is a spark escaping from a bonfire, and Gabe and I were the sun, burning hot enough to light the world.

Suddenly, I can't stand to be in Isaac's arms another second. Tonight, making love isn't enough. I need to get out. I roll to one side, sending Isaac's limp cock sliding from my body, eager to wipe the stickiness from between my legs.

"Go back to sleep," I whisper as I drop my feet to the cool hardwood floor beside the bed, and reach for tissues from the box on the bedside table. "I'm going for a run."

"I'll come with you," Isaac says, sitting up.

"I'd rather go alone." I toss the tissues in the trash and grab a sports bra from my top dresser door. I tug it on, shifting my tee shirt up around my neck to fit my arms through the bra straps before pulling it back on and reaching for a pair of gym shorts.

"That woman was abducted right off the highway not far from here," Isaac says. "It's not safe for you to go out by yourself in the middle of the night."

"I'm careful. I stick to the back roads," I say. "No one ever sees me."

"I'm coming with you," Isaac says in his stubborn voice. "I spent half of last week filing reports on the guys they think might have taken the girl. I've got a better idea of what kind of scum live around here than you do."

I doubt it, I think, but I don't say the words aloud.

A few months ago, Isaac applied to join the Maui P.D. and was accepted into the police academy. Just last week, he started work full time at the station in Kahului. He's already making friends and impressing his superiors, but he's still new on the job. He hasn't had time to do his research, to look into our community's dark corners and take notes on what the bad guys have been up to.

I, however, have three binders full of material on possible targets. Information I've cobbled together from the mothers at the school, the ladies who gossip down at the local pool during open swim, and the bits and pieces I overhear on Isaac's police scanner. I've got intimate details on a shipping mogul who's helping smuggle underage mail order brides into the country for his buddies. I have the names and addresses of fathers who are delinquent on their child support, spending their money on motorcycles and beer, while their children walk around in Salvation Army flip flops two sizes too big. I even have an inch-thick file on a sexual predator in Makawao, who attacked a girl last month, only a few weeks after he was released from prison.

Late at night, when I can't sleep, I fantasize about the jobs I could pull here if Gabe and I were still partners in crime. I think about the people we could help, and the rush of moving silently through the darkness dressed in my blacks, adrenaline coursing through my veins.

If Isaac knew the things I daydream about, he would be horrified. Isaac doesn't believe in vigilantism and would never support anyone breaking the law. He wouldn't have been okay with me taking the law into my own hands before he was a cop, and he certainly wouldn't be okay with it now. He would throw my lock picking set into the sea, burn my blacks, and forbid me from even thinking about indulging that side of myself ever again. Hell, he might even leave. I know Isaac loves me, but I'm not sure how long his love would last if he ever opened up his eyes and looked at the big picture.

Isaac loves the Caitlin he's created. He loves the palatable pieces he's pasted together, not the complete person, and that's why our relationship will never be as real as what I had with Gabe. I'm keeping too many secrets, secrets that keep me isolated, sad, and longing for something I'll never have again.

I will never meet another man like Gabe, a man who is ruthless, but kind, lawless, but true to his own code. A man who can kill a monster without remorse, and still spend an hour in a petting zoo with a two-year-old girl on a hundred degree day, dripping sweat until his shirt's soaked through because he refuses to force her away from the baby bunnies. A man who will admire my love for my family, and my taste for breaking the law, and love me better because both of those things exist inside the same person.

I know some people find true love more than once, but I think they must be better than I am. They must be people with soft edges, who can easily shift and slide and reshape themselves until they fit with someone new. I am not soft. I am hard and my edges are chiseled in stone, hammered out in a craggy shoreline only one ship could ever sail through without getting smashed against the rocks.

Hard. Hard. Hard. Made to slice or shatter.

The mantra drums through my head as Isaac and I slip out of the house and hit the darkened streets, jogging down our gravel country lane before turning onto the narrow road that leads toward the town grocery store, the community center, and the school, where the kids are doing so well.

Sean has dozens of new friends, Ray is the top reader in his class—and the librarian's pet—and Danny has been keeping out of trouble and getting decent grades for the first time in his life. He even has a girlfriend, a sweetheart named Sam with a raunchy sense of humor who loves skateboarding as much as Danny, and is teaching him how to surf. My family is thriving, and I'm well on my way to getting a college degree. I have a boyfriend who loves me, an adorable house, and no worries about making rent, or paying my bills. *And* I live on a tropical island where it's warm enough to go jogging in the middle of the night three hundred and sixty-five days a year.

I should be melting into a puddle of contentment, but I'm not.

I am hard, and I prove it by pushing Isaac to the limit during our run. After the police academy, he's in better shape than back when he played football in high school, but despite his longer legs, he has a hard time keeping up with me. Since I lost the baby, I've run almost every day, and I've gotten fast. Fast enough to join the college track team if I wanted, fast enough that Isaac has to struggle to keep pace when I'm going full out.

I know he's suffering by the end of the first mile, but I don't slow down. I push and push, until sweat is dripping down my forehead into my eyes, and Isaac is pulling in hoarse, labored breaths beside me, and still, I don't ease up.

I keep running like my future depends on it, even though I know I will never be able to run far enough, or fast enough, to escape the ghost of the love I lost.

CHAPTER SEVENTEEN

GABE

"Tis in my memory lock'd...shall keep..."

"Wider, I want to see every inch." I stare down at the nude girl on the bed angled into the corner of her cramped studio apartment, watching as she spreads her tanned thighs wide, baring the slick pink flesh between her legs.

"Touch yourself," I say, reaching down to stroke my cock with one hand, keeping myself hard. "Show me how you make yourself come."

"But I...don't do that," the girl says, blushing.

"Now you do," I say, seriously doubting that a twenty-five year old cocktail waitress who agreed to take me home without much more than a crook of my finger has never masturbated. "Touch yourself. I want you to come on your hand before I fuck you with my mouth."

The girl's breath shudders out and her nipples tighten as she dips her fingers between her legs. Her eyes slide closed as she begins to stroke herself with a confidence that confirms my theory that she was only playing innocent.

Her lie makes me even less inclined to remember her name.

Her name doesn't matter. She is what she is.

She's Wednesday night's girl, another blonde, but different than the blonde I was fucking last week, or the week before. I don't keep any of them around for long. None of them hold my interest, because none of them are Caitlin, the girl I loved, the one who has vanished without a trace. When the memories first started coming back, I thought maybe I'd actually seen her that day at the airport, but once I learned more about her history, I realized that must have been wishful thinking, my damaged brain projecting the image of a girl I didn't yet know I was searching for.

Since then, I've broken the Internet looking for her, but I can't find a phone number, an address, or a social media page. Not even an abandoned Facebook page from high school. There is a link to an article in the local paper from years ago, naming Caitlin as one of the scholarship winners receiving a full ride to Christoph Academy, and nothing else. It's like she dropped off the face of the earth the day she dropped out of school to raise her sister's baby, and so far, none of the memories I've recaptured give me any clue where she might have gone.

But I'm going to find her. My memories are fuzzy and full of holes, but I am painting a more complete picture of last summer with every passing day. Fragments of memory flash on my mental screen, like scraps of film plucked from the cutting room floor. Piece by piece, they are filling in the blanks, confirming I am an even worse person than I suspected in the early days after the surgery.

I didn't just fuck around and lie to everyone who loved me, I made a hobby out of breaking and entering. I stole thousands of dollars' worth of merchandise that I put through a fence in Charleston, even though I have a trust fund worth millions and more money coming the day my aging grandmother passes away. I robbed people for fun, I suppose. I don't know for sure.

I don't know who I used to be, or why I did the things I did, I only know that this helps. Fucking takes me closer to the memories. When I'm rock hard, and balls deep, riding this week's blonde like this night is the last I'll ever have, the lid on my memories creaks open and the past comes buzzing out. The rush of sweat and heated blood and orgasm sends me swinging out over the edge of the chasm left behind by the surgery, showing me some of what is waiting on the other side.

Two nights ago, I recaptured thirty seconds of Caitlin standing in the shadows across from a farmhouse. I was walking softly through the trees behind her. She didn't know I was watching as she pulled on her black leather gloves and smoothed a knit mask over her head. She didn't know I tracked her fingers as she tucked her hair beneath the mask with graceful movements that made me certain she was going to be an elegant thief.

I've seen Caitlin in my memories enough to know that we committed crimes together, even if I don't know why, or where she's gone. When the memories started trickling in last January, I convinced Olia to drive me by Caitlin's house, wheedling at my nurse until she consented to violate my mother's "no going into town without a parent" rule for something other than a trip to the pizza parlor. Back then, I was still using a cane, but I left it in the van, forcing myself to stand tall as I climbed the steps to Caitlin's front door, my heart slamming in my chest as I realized I might be seconds away from seeing her again.

But Caitlin wasn't there. Her father met me at the door to their sagging ranch house, leaning against the doorframe with his thick arms crossed over his stomach, making it clear I wasn't welcome inside. He said he hadn't seen Caitlin since last summer, shortly before he received a call from his oldest son, Danny, saying that the rest of the kids needed help because Caitlin had run away. I asked where his other children were, and Chuck said he'd taken them to Florida to live with his younger sister. None of them wanted to stay in Giffney, not after being abandoned by yet another person who had promised to be there for them.

He wasn't friendly, but he wasn't unfriendly, either, and I had no reason to believe he was lying. From what I remember, Chuck and I hated each other. If he had known where Caitlin was, I'm sure he would have enjoyed shoving the information in my face. He legitimately seemed to think his daughter had tired of the drudgery of raising four kids and run off, the way her mother and sister had before her.

But I remember the way Caitlin looked at those kids. I remember thinking she'd be an amazing mother and that maybe—if things had been different—she and I might have had a child together, a life together. But things weren't different, and for some reason she vanished, and I don't know why, and it kills me a little more every day.

I have to know what happened, I have to find the missing pieces before I lose what's left of my mind.

"That's good enough," I say to the blonde on the bed as her breath grows harsh and uneven, stopping her seemingly moments before her busy fingers bring her over the edge.

"But I—"

"Turn over," I order as I join her on the bed. I roll on a condom as I move, deciding I don't want to get my tongue between her legs, after all. I can smell that she wouldn't taste like peaches dipped in the ocean. She wouldn't taste like Caitlin, and I can't stand to have another woman's taste in my mouth.

"Turn over," I repeat when the woman takes a second too long. "I want your ass in the air."

The blonde nods and scrambles to do my bidding, and I hate it.

I hate the way her pink claws dig into the pillow in front of her as she lifts her ass and spreads her legs. I hate the happy whimper she makes as I grip her hips and drive, hard and fast, into her slick channel. I hate the way she bounces her ass back against my cock as we establish an urgent rhythm and pound toward the edge together.

I hate her, not because she deserves to be hated, but because she isn't Caitlin. Caitlin, who handed over the reins to her pleasure with a steady hand, and wasn't afraid to call me an asshole even as she parted her lips and sucked me off exactly the way I told her to. Caitlin, who submitted the way she did everything else, with pride, honesty, and so much heart you could feel her passion pulsing in the air with every breath she took.

Now, I close my eyes and hold my breath, not wanting to see or smell this stranger. This is simply a means to an end, a way to reach out and touch the razor sharp edges of my lost memories, even though it hurts.

Because it hurts.

I want to hurt. I want to feel alive again.

I want to feel the way I felt when I was with her.

I fuck harder, faster, focusing on the pressure building low in my body, the way my muscles heat and my spine vibrates with the orgasm that is so close, so close. Fuck...I'm so close. I clench my jaw and pump faster, until skin slaps against skin and I'm hurtling toward the edge so quickly I couldn't stop if I tried.

My orgasm hits like running into a brick wall. Stars explode behind my closed eyes. There is a flash of orange light and then I see a room with a single bulb hanging from the ceiling. I see a stained mattress in the corner, and taste fury on my tongue. I'm so enraged it feels like the ligaments stretched over my clenched fists are going to snap free of the bone. I smell burning rubber and sulfur and a hundred foul things. I am so filled with hate I'm almost blind with it, and when the memory comes I catch only flashes— my hands wrapped around someone's neck, a mouth parted in a silent scream, eyes bulging with terror, and then a wave of pain so intense even the memory of it makes me wince.

The memory world goes black as I am blinded by the pain, but I can feel the way the person I'm straddling struggles as they fight for life. I feel slim ribs contract as I clench a body between my thighs, determined to crush the person beneath me to pieces.

After a few breathless moments, my orgasm ebbs away, taking the dark memory with it. My eyes crack open, but I don't see the girl catching her breath in front of me. I see the web of my own lashes and the blurred edges of my nose. I pull in a deep breath, grateful it's over, but as I slide my spent cock from the blonde's body, another image flashes through my mind. It is Caitlin's face and she is as beautiful as ever, but crying like the world is ending. Her arms are wrapped tight around her narrow ribs, her face is blotchy and red, and when she turns her head to one side, I see that her neck is covered in bruises that bloom blue, black, and yellow against her pale skin.

I sit back on my heels, shaking all over, suddenly as weak as I was during those first marathon physical therapy sessions, when I was determined to bend my body to my will if I couldn't bend my mind. I don't want to put together the pieces of what I saw, but I can't stop my brain from chugging down the tracks toward the obvious conclusion.

Bruises on Caitlin's throat; my hands wrapped around someone's neck. Caitlin's arms cradling her ribs; my thighs contracting, crushing the slim chest I have pinned beneath me. Caitlin gone, vanished without a trace, only a few nights before I suddenly changed my mind about the surgery and fled South Carolina with my parents.

I don't remember what changed my mind about having the operation when I was so dead set against it, but it must have been something big. Something so big that having my brain carved full of holes and rolling the dice on being a vegetable for the rest of my life seemed like a decent idea. Something I had to run from because I couldn't stand to stay and face what I'd done.

God... Could I...

Could I have hurt her? Maybe even...

"No." The word hurts as it claws its way free of my throat. I don't want to believe I'm capable of hurting someone I loved as much as I loved Caitlin, but I've remembered enough to know I wasn't a nice guy last summer.

Hell, I'm not a nice guy now. I've been fucking my way through the single women in Giffney like it's my job. I lie to my parents, and I'm certain they're lying to me, even though hacking into their email hasn't revealed that they are anything but devoted to my happiness. I am arrogant, blunt to the point of rudeness, bitter, jaded—basically an asshole, who doesn't deserve the amazing luck I've had.

But there's a big difference between being an asshole, and a murderer.

"Are you okay?"

I look up to find the blonde has turned to face me. Her hand rests lightly on my bare thigh and her blue eyes are filled with concern.

"I'm fine." I snap the condom off and toss it in the wastebasket by the bed, wanting to stand up and get the hell out of here, but my knees are still too unsteady.

"It's hot in here, isn't it? Do you want to take a shower while I make us some margaritas?" the blonde asks in a hopeful voice that makes me hate her more than I did before. "Something frozen always helps cool me down."

206

I don't say a word. I look into her face, into those eyes so eager to please a man who's treated her like dirt beneath his shoe from the moment I told her she was taking me home when she got off work, and I am filled with loathing. I loathe her, and I loathe myself, and together it is the worst feeling. It is a dark, hopeless, terrible feeling, but it isn't enough to make me want to put my hands around her throat.

I don't want to hurt her, not even a little bit, and the knowledge helps me pull my shit together.

"No, thank you," I say in a gentler tone than any I've used with her so far. "I have to go. I'm... not myself." *Whoever that is.* "I'm sorry."

"It's okay." Her eyes squint with concern, drawing my attention to the mascara smudged beneath her lashes. Even with her makeup running down her face and her curls frizzing, she's a beautiful woman. Kind, too. She deserves better than a one-night stand with a man who couldn't give less of a shit about her.

"Is there anything I can do?" she asks. "To make you feel better?"

I shake my head as I stand and begin pulling on my clothes with swift, jerky motions.

"You don't have to run off." She crosses her arms and tucks her tanned legs beneath her. "I'm not scared of a little dark stuff."

"How about a lot of dark stuff," I mumble, the words out before I decide to speak them.

She cocks her head, studying me, her clear eyes big and wide, but not as innocent looking as they were before. "I don't know. Depends. I had a husband who used to rough me up. I'm not into that."

"I'm not into that, either," I say, praying that it's true.

"I know." She smiles a shy smile that seems out of place considering we've already fucked. "You're bossy, but harmless."

I grunt, wishing I could agree with her, but I can't. I'm not sure that I'm harmless, and I know I don't deserve the kindness in her voice.

"I should go." I turn and cross the room, throwing my parting words over my shoulder. "I'm not good company right now."

"I don't need good company," she calls after me. "I just want someone who will fuck me like a house on fire and not tell me how to live my life."

I pause at the door, the handle in my hand.

"I'm not looking for a boyfriend," she continues. "I've had enough of those to last a lifetime. I just want to have some fun and…I had fun tonight. With you."

"I don't even remember your name," I confess.

"It's Kimmy," she says, laughing. "I don't mind people forgetting. It's a stupid name."

"Why do you say that?" I still don't turn around, not sure I'm up for even a fuck-buddy level of commitment.

"It's a bimbo name." I hear the mattress squeak and when she speaks again her voice is closer. "I'm going to change it as soon as my mom dies. I would do it now, but I don't want to hurt her feelings."

I turn, unable to keep my eyes from tracking up and down her nude form, admiring her slim legs and large breasts with the dusky nipples. She's gorgeous, but her eyes don't look like the eyes of a girl who wants a no-strings-attached relationship. Kimmy is looking for love, whether she realizes it or not, and I'm definitely not in the market.

"You seem like a nice girl," I say. "But I—"

"I'm four years older than you," she says, giggling, her smile making her even prettier. "You can boss me around in bed, but you don't get to call me a girl, college boy."

My lips curve the slightest bit. It isn't a smile, but it's closer than I've come to one in a long time.

Suddenly, I don't hate Kimmy, and I hate myself a tiny bit less.

"I thought you might have a nice smile." She grins. "Come on, let's have a drink and hang out. No pressure, just good times."

"Why don't we get out of here, instead," I say, deciding there are worse ways to spend the rest of the evening, like going home and trying to sleep while Caitlin's brutalized body flashes behind my closed eyes. "We could get burgers and beers?"

Her eyes light up. "Sounds perfect. Give me two minutes to freshen up."

She disappears through a curtain of glass beads that leads into her closet and the bathroom on the other side. There's no door on the john, and I can hear her peeing and running water to wash her hands, hear her humming as she fixes her makeup. The sounds are intimate sounds, and for a moment I feel less alone.

The realization makes me reach for the door again.

I deserve to feel alone, I deserve to suffer and ache until I find out the truth, until I know if I hurt the woman I loved, or if I'm reading the clues all wrong.

Please let me be reading them wrong. Please, if there is a God, let this be okay.

Let Caitlin still be alive.

"You ready?" Kimmy swishes back through the beads before I can make a break for the stairs. Her frizzy hair has been smoothed into slightly damp curls, and her smudged mascara replaced by black liner that makes her eyes look even bigger.

"Ready," I say, forcing a smile as I open the door for her.

I don't deserve a stress-free night, but I need one. I need to put the horrible images I saw tonight aside before they drive me crazy. I'll add them to the rest of my clues, close the lid on the puzzle, and wait until I have enough pieces to form a complete picture.

Or you could quit before it's too late, move on with your life before you learn something that will ruin your second chance.

The thought teases through my brain as Kimmy and I file down the three stories of stairs to the ground floor of her building, one of the oldest in historic downtown. A long time ago The Merrylark was a hotel, then a rooming house for men working in the textile plant, and now it houses apartments that are supposed to be funky and retro, but from what I've seen are simply cramped and poorly designed.

But the building is centrally located, right across the street from Harry's twenty-four hour diner, two blocks from the old courthouse and central library, and just a block from The Neptune, a Greek restaurant that serves burgers and fries, as well as traditional Greek fair.

"How about Harry's?" Kimmy asks as we emerge onto the sidewalk and are swallowed into the humid heat of the July night.

I glance across the street at the neon sign flickering above the diner and feel a tickle at the base of my brain. Another memory rises inside of me—something about the diner, something that happened there, something to do with Caitlin—but I banish it with a shake of my head.

"No, let's go to The Neptune," I say. "They've got colder beer."

I have no idea if that's true, but it's as good an excuse as any not to go into Harry's. I don't want to face any more memories tonight. Or maybe tomorrow night, either. Maybe the gutless voice in my head is right, and I should quit fighting to reconstruct last summer before it's too late. I've never considered myself a coward before, but now...

The image of Caitlin's bruise-mottled neck and tear-streaked face drifts through my mind again, but then Kimmy takes my hand and starts telling me a story about when she was little and her mom would take her for midnight breakfast, and the image fades away, replaced by Kimmy's blue eyes and open smile. By the time we push through the door to The Neptune, and are enveloped in the smell of garlic, fried meat, and mint, there is nothing but the present and a girl who seems to want to help me put the past behind me.

CHAPTER EIGHTEEN

CAITLIN

Two weeks later...

*"What is genius, but the power
of expressing a new individuality?"*
-Elizabeth Barrett Browning

*J*ust after four o'clock in the morning, I slip through the window and drop quietly to the ground outside Mr. Munroe's five thousand square foot mansion. It's an hour later than I planned—the sleeping pills I tucked into the meat took longer to knock out his dogs than I anticipated—but I have plenty of time to get back home before Isaac and the kids get up. I'm still on track to pulling off this job without getting caught, and have no reason to be worried.

And then I hear it, a soft growl near the damaged portion of the fence, where I eased into the backyard ten minutes ago, on my way to steal Mr. Munroe's hard drive.

I freeze, my pulse spiking and my mouth filling with a sour, metallic taste. I hold completely still, straining my ears, praying they were playing tricks on me, but then it comes again, a low growl, closer this time. I scan the darkness in front of me, but I can't see a damned thing. The moon has gone behind the clouds and Munroe's yard is dotted with palm and fruit trees. There are shadows everywhere, dozens of places for a pissed off, drugged up dog to hide.

I take a slow step backward that's greeted with another growl. Seconds later, a small, compact silhouette staggers out from beneath the inky blackness beneath an orange tree ten feet away. It's the smaller dog, the one that barked the loudest when I first appeared at the fence shortly after midnight.

The sleeping pills should have knocked both of the pit bulls out for hours, but maybe the bigger one got greedy and ate more than his share of hamburger. Or maybe the little guy has a super powered metabolism and has already burned through his dose. Whichever is to blame, it doesn't matter. The dog is awake and ready to defend its territory. Now, I just have to hope it's still sufficiently drugged for me to have a shot at outrunning it before it gets a mouthful of my leg.

Moving slowly, I tuck the bag containing the hard drive down the front of my pants, knowing I'll want both arms free for my dash toward the front gate. I came in through the crack in the fence, but it took time for me to squeeze through. Now, I don't have time. I'll have to make a run down the driveway and jump the gate.

There are cameras monitoring the front drive, but I'm wearing my blacks. Munroe shouldn't be able to see any identifiable characteristics when he reviews the footage. And maybe—once he realizes that I've taken the hard drive containing the pictures he's been using to blackmail a local elementary school teacher, *and* pictures of Munroe, one of Maui's most upstanding county councilmen, in the middle of a circle jerk with two of his oldest male friends—he'll decide against contacting the police.

A girl can only hope, because I have no doubt that if Isaac saw the surveillance footage, he would be able to make me in a second, even with my entire body and face covered in black knit. Isaac knows the way I move, the way I jump, the way I pump my arms when I'm sprinting the last half mile of a run. He'll know me if he sees me, but the thought doesn't make me alter my technique as I turn and bolt for the front of the house, the dog's claws scrabbling on the ground as it starts after me.

I need to haul ass and I'm not about to alter the technique that makes me faster than Isaac, faster than Danny, maybe even faster than Gabe if he were still alive.

I cling to the thought, imagining Gabe's voice cheering me on, telling me I can make it, telling me to fucking run like my life depends on it, as I race toward the front gate. Behind me, the dog's growl has become a bark loud enough to wake the dead. Munroe is going to be out of bed any minute. If the dog gets its teeth into me, it won't be long before Munroe is out on the lawn, ready to rip off my mask and find out who broke into his house.

I can't let the dog catch up. I have to run faster.

I haul ass, arms pumping, ribs heaving as I draw deep, ragged breaths, fueling the muscles in my legs that are straining forward with everything they've got. By the time I reach the end of the drive, my lungs feel like they're going to explode, but I make it without getting chomped.

I extend both arms and leap for the top of the thick, wooden gate, grateful it isn't one that opens automatically when approached from the inside. I am almost out of sprint power and the dog is close enough that I can feel its breath hot on my ankles as I swing my legs up and over. I land on the other side of the gate in a less-than-graceful tangle of arms and legs, but I'm up and on my feet in seconds.

Knowing there's no time to catch my breath, I turn and bolt down the darkened country road, heading away from the trail I used to get here, even though it's the shortest route back to the house. But so far I've always kept true to Gabe's signature job style—in and out in no more than ten minutes, always have at least three routes plotted beforehand, and never use the same route twice.

By the time I reach the Hana Highway, the only major road leading to the east side of the island, a light rain is falling and my leg muscles are trembling, but I don't let myself slow down until I am across the road and deep into the field of grass on the other side. Only then do I stop for a second and tilt my head back, lifting my face to the cool rain. The drops kiss my closed lids and hot cheeks, slipping between my parted lips to leave the taste of clean, island water on my tongue.

I take a deep breath in and out, overcome with gratitude. I'm grateful to live in a place where the rain tastes like flowers and fresh sea air. I'm grateful that I took a chance and started pulling jobs on my own and that I'm doing my small part to make people's lives better here.

And I'm grateful as hell that I didn't get caught.

I love this island, but it's smaller than it seems when you first arrive. A person can only go so far before they run into a beach or a jungle or a volcanic crater with no road leading to the other side. Sooner or later, I'm going to have to stop pulling jobs or take the breaking and entering elsewhere, otherwise there will be no issue of whether I'll get caught, only when.

The thought is a sobering one, and by the time I reach the house forty minutes later, I am more subdued than I usually am after a job. I ease into the shed and deposit the hard drive under the loose board in the corner. I slip out of my blacks and shove them into the hole next to the hard drive, making a mental note to wash them while Isaac's at work, and change into my running clothes.

I've just slotted the board back into place and am heading back out of the shed—planning to take a very short jog around the neighborhood before creeping in the back door to the house—when the door flies open, revealing Danny on the other side.

"Shit," I curse, my hand flying to cover my heart. "You scared me."

"Isaac's been up for two hours," Danny says in a low voice. "He was in the bathroom when I saw you come across the lawn, but he knows something is up."

I swallow and force a smile, ignoring the way my pulse leaps at my throat. "I went for a long run and got lost. It's no big deal."

Danny watches me for a long moment, and his pale green eyes—so like mine, from the color, to the thick fringe of lashes, to the old-before-his-time look that flickers behind them when he's thinking—study me in the dim light.

Finally, he whispers, "Is everything okay?"

I nod, fake smile vanishing. "Yes. Everything is fine. I promise."

"I get that you have things you need to do…" Danny sighs, glancing back over his shoulder toward the house before he turns back to me. "But if you're going to keep it up, you've got to get rid of Isaac."

"You love Isaac," I say, chest aching at how calm Danny sounds when talking about getting rid of a friend who has become like family to us in the past few months.

"I love you more," Danny says. "And he's not like Gabe, Caitlin. If he finds out about any of it, even the stuff that happened before we moved, he's not going to be cool."

"Let me worry about Isaac," I say, hating that I've done such a shitty job of protecting Danny, and anxious that maybe I haven't been as successful at hiding my illicit activities as I've thought. If Danny knows, Isaac must at least suspect something, though I doubt he'd make the leap to breaking and entering without some sort of evidence.

"Seriously, don't worry," I add as I cross the shed to rest a hand on his shoulder, surprised to realize I have to reach up a little to do it. "Just be a kid for a little while longer, okay? Let the grown-ups handle the grown-up stuff."

"I haven't been a kid for a long time," Danny says, in a matter of fact way that makes it hard to chalk the statement up to teenage angst. "And I don't want to lose this. Things are good here. I don't want Isaac to screw that up."

"I'm the one who would screw it up," I say softly, a wave of self-loathing rushing through me as I cross my arms at my chest. "Isaac's not the problem, I am, and I'm sorry. I promise I'll try to do better."

"But you have been doing better," Danny says. "That's the thing. Whatever you've been doing lately, when you go running late at night, makes you better. I get that. And I'd rather you do whatever you need to do than watch you zone out staring at the wall with tears running down your face. I hated that. I hated when you came home from the hospital all numb and sad and nothing we did could make you better."

I blink, surprised by the intensity in my brother's voice. "I'm sorry," I say again, feeling like more of a failure with every passing second.

"Don't be sorry, just don't get caught," he adds, pushing his long blond hair—almost long enough to get into a ponytail like the older surfers he admires—from his face. "I love you, okay?"

"I love you, too," I say, pulling him into my arms for a hug.

He resists for a minute, but then his wiry arms close around me and he hugs me hard. We stand that way for a long minute, until the back door to the house opens and Isaac calls my name.

"I'm here." I pull away from Danny, holding my brother's eyes for a beat, silently promising to take care of things, before I turn and cross the lawn.

And I will take care of things.

I won't let anything hurt the people I love, not even me.

CHAPTER NINETEEN

CAITLIN

"He said true things, but
called them by wrong names."
-Elizabeth Barrett Browning

Isaac stands on the back lanai, dressed in his running clothes, his thick arms crossed at his chest and a frown creasing his once perpetually cheery face. My best friend says that the day I agreed to be his girlfriend was the best day of his life, but I've seen him scowl more in the past few months than in all our years of friendship combined.

"Where have you been?" he asks, his voice rough, earning him a hard look from Danny as my brother heads into the house. "I've been worried sick."

"I'm sorry," I say, shutting the door behind Danny, figuring it's best if Isaac and I stay outside so none of the kids can hear us fighting. "I went running, and ended up down by the beach. I started watching the waves and just...lost track of time."

Isaac shakes his head, and the frown wrinkling his broad forehead deepens. "That's not okay, Caitlin. You can't go running off and stay gone for hours without telling anyone where you're going. There are people here who care about you, and who get fucking worried when you disappear in the middle of the night."

"I was fine, Isaac." I ignore the irritation that flickers in my chest. Isaac cares, that's why he's worried, and I'm sure I'd be concerned if the shoe were on the other foot. "I know you think it's dangerous for me to go running alone, but I promise you, I can take care of myself."

"I seriously doubt that, Caitlin," he snaps, his tone as harsh as it was the night he told me he thought Gabe was turning me into a callous, unfeeling person. "You've been one step away from falling apart for months. I know it, the kids know it, even Sherry knows it. We're all just waiting for you to go running one night and never come back."

Now it's my turn to scowl. "That's not fair, Isaac. It's been a tough year, but the kids are doing great in school, and so am I. And if Sherry's worried, she hasn't said anything to me. She seemed fine when we hung out last weekend."

"She's afraid to upset you," Isaac says. "It's me she calls when you forget to show up for a coffee date, or blow off dinner without calling to reschedule."

"I've done each of those things exactly once," I say, propping my hands on my hips. "And I told her I was sorry. I got busy studying and spaced about dinner, and the time I missed coffee was the day I had to sign the kids up for swim lessons. I was in line longer than I thought I would be, and didn't have cell service to call and let her know I—"

"Make all the excuses you want," Isaac says, cutting me off. "But I know something's not right with you. You haven't been yourself since you started dating Gabe, and it's only gotten worse since you lost the baby."

I flinch. We never talk about the baby. We never talk about anything that happened between when I started dating Gabe, and the day Isaac moved to the island. That parcel of time has been mutually declared off limits. Isaac doesn't want to hear about it, and I don't want to share the private memories of my time with Gabe with anyone, not even my best friend.

But Isaac is more than my best friend now. He's my boyfriend, my lover, and I should be able to trust him with every piece of me, but I don't. And that is part of the reason I've been so long coming back to myself. Standing here, looking up at him, seeing the judgment on his face, I realize that I've been living up to his opinion of me. Every day, I see a reflection of the fragile girl Isaac thinks I am in my partner's eyes, and that reflection is as unhealthy as living in the past, longing for a man I'll never see again.

Both of those things have to change, or I'll have to end it with Isaac. Not because he might one day catch me doing something illegal, but because he won't let me be the person I am now, instead of the overwhelmed girl I was when we were growing up, or the broken woman he found when he first stepped off the plane last fall.

We're going to have to have a long, hard talk and decide whether or not we can give each other room to breathe, grow, and change, but not this morning. I'm too tired to face that kind of talk, and I need to get the younger kids up and ready for Friday morning swim lessons.

I'd like to talk to Sherry before I approach Isaac, too, and see what she thinks. No matter what Isaac says, the last time we had dinner in

Paia—the cute hippy town where Sherry lives with her boyfriend, Bjorn—I didn't sense that she was upset or worried. If anything, she's been the one who's been distant, so obsessed with her first true love that she barely has time to come to dinner at the house anymore.

I make a mental note to call Sherry while I'm sitting in the bleachers watching Sean and Emmie splash around in the pool, and step past Isaac into the house, not bothering to address his last statement.

"So that's it?" he calls after me as I move into the kitchen and grab a bottle of water from the fridge. "Aren't we going to finish this conversation?"

"I am finished," I say in a tone I haven't heard come out of my mouth in a long time. It's a strong, grounded tone, and I know what I did tonight is partially responsible.

By stealing that hard drive, I helped save a young woman's career and put her future back in her own hands. As soon as Mimi has the incriminating pictures in her possession, she'll have more than enough material to tell Skip Munroe that their affair is over, and that he'd better keep his distance if he doesn't want erotic photos of him and his buddies leaked to the press. She will never again have to put up with being blackmailed or used by a man who once swore he loved her.

I know how free she's going to feel because it's the same way I felt last summer, when Gabe and I made our third deposit into my college fund and I realized I was going to have enough money to get a college education, and break the cycle of poverty that had plagued my family for generations. Pulling jobs isn't just about the rush I feel when I pick a lock or get in and out without getting caught, it's about the rush of knowing I'm helping someone the law has let down, tipping the scales of justice back in the favor of those who wouldn't have a fair shake any other way.

"Great," Isaac says, his tone making it clear things are anything but great between us. "Then I'm going for a run, and don't expect me back anytime soon."

I turn to tell him he should enjoy himself, and stay gone as long as he wants to, but he's already slamming out the back door. I watch him storm across the yard through the window above the sink, with a sigh. I have a feeling I'm going to be making Isaac mad a lot in the next few weeks, but I'm not going to back down.

I don't want to be the girl made of glass anymore. I want to be strong—the woman Gabe was certain could handle anything life threw in her path.

CHAPTER TWENTY

CAITLIN

"*D*o you think Isaac is going for good?" Danny asks, sticking his head into the kitchen from where he's obviously been eavesdropping in the hall.

I shake my head. "No. He's just upset. He'll be back by dinner time." I put the cap on my bottle of water and stick it back in the fridge. "Could you go wake up Sean and Emmie?" I ask, turning back to Danny. "We have to be at the pool by seven, and I want them to have time to eat and let their food settle for at least thirty minutes before they get in the water."

Danny snorts. "That's not even a real thing. I ate two cheeseburgers ten minutes before I went surfing yesterday, and I was fine."

"It is so a real thing," I say. "And you'd better

wait at least twenty minutes next time. No one else is allowed to die on my watch, okay?"

The smartass twist to Danny's lips flattens into a tight line. "Okay. Do you want Ray up, too?"

"No, he can sleep in. You're going to be at the house until you and Sam leave for the movies this afternoon right?"

Danny nods. "And Ray can come with us if he wants. Sam's little brother is coming. Her parents are gone all day on some crater hike, and they don't want her leaving Erick alone."

"Cool," I say, proud of the person Danny's becoming. "I bet Ray would like that."

"Whatever." Danny shrugs. "Gotta get him out of the house every once in a while. No one should spend that much time reading inside when there's a beach ten minutes from their house. It's like, against the natural order of the universe."

"I appreciate your devotion to the natural order of the universe," I say with a smile. "And I love you a lot."

Danny rolls his eyes, but as he leaves the room, he mumbles that he loves me, too. His voice is soft, but loud enough to hear, and it makes my smile stretch a little wider. It's been a hell of a year, but when the going gets tough,

Danny and I are still there for each other. We've made it through a lot of hard times in the past without much help, and if we have to, we can make it without Isaac.

I love Isaac, but in the long run it might be less hurtful to end things now, instead of a year or two down the road, when I'm fed up pretending to be someone I'm not, and Isaac is miserable because I won't stay in the box he wants to put me in. The thought is a sad one—I'll never love Isaac the way I loved Gabe, but I doubt I'll ever care about another man the way I care about Isaac—but I put it away for now.

Sufficient to the day is the misery thereof. It's something my grandmother used to say, and a bit of wisdom I've been thinking about a lot lately. Taken all at once, the misery of the past twelve months might break me, but if I take each day's challenges one at a time, I can make it through, and maybe even start to heal the bruised places on my heart.

As Danny moves around on the opposite side of the house, waking Emmie and carrying her into the hall bathroom to use the potty before she gets her swimsuit on, I cross to the kitchen table and open my laptop. I always mean to take it upstairs to my desk, but it ends up hanging out next to me for almost every meal. It's amazing how much studying I can squeeze in while shoveling salad and tuna poke into my mouth.

I open up my email, wanting to make sure that swim lessons aren't cancelled the way they were two weeks ago when Emmie's teacher called in sick, and am greeted with a string of new emails, all three from Chuck.

My stomach transforms into a stress knot at the center of my body and I suddenly wish I'd skipped the email check until later in the day. A bunch of emails from Chuck never mean good news, and I prefer not to manage correspondence from my father until I've had at least two strong cups of coffee.

The last time Chuck sent a string of messages, it was to tell me—in three epic emails filled with so many spelling mistakes it was clear they were written while he was three sheets to the wind—that he wouldn't be flying in to spend Christmas with the kids, after all, due to some bullshit with Veronica and her daughter. The time before that, he sent me a handful of messages, most of them featuring links to websites devoted to dealing with grief, and one email in all lowercase letters musing that maybe it was for the best that Gabe's baby joined his daddy in heaven so that I didn't have to be a single mother raising a kid on my own.

That particular email made me hurl my phone against the wall, and only the super tough case Sherry had bought me, when I ruined my first phone at the beach our first week on the island, kept it from shattering to pieces.

Isaac insisted that Chuck had meant well, but I knew better.

I could see the smug grin hidden between his consoling remarks and lazy, lowercase letters. For whatever reason—an intense dislike of Gabe, or his own selfish desire not to be saddled with any more grandchildren—Chuck was glad I lost the baby. Aside from giving me the house, the kindest thing Chuck has done in the past year was to keep his distance. If I never see him again, I wouldn't shed a tear, and if I never have to open another email from his *irisheyesrsmiling* address, I would consider my life the better for it.

I almost shut the laptop and postpone my torment, but in the end I decide I'd rather take my punishment and know what Chuck's up to rather than have Unknown Awful hanging over my head all day.

I click on the oldest message to find another long, lowercase ramble filled with typos. I skim the email, gathering from the mess that Chuck has something weighing on his mind, something he needs to explain and get off his chest before he goes to the hospital.

The mention of the hospital is unexpected, but I'm not worried. Chuck's been in the hospital before, usually because of some drunken tumble down a set of stairs, or the result of passing out on the street between the bar and home, and getting frostbite by the time he woke up the next morning.

I click on the second email to see only six words—I'M SO SORRY PLEASE BELIEVE ME—all in caps as if he'd tried to make up for using only lowercase in the first email. I sigh, wondering what he's sorry for this time, and open the final and latest email, expecting to find the mystery solved and Chuck's latest sin spelled out.

Instead, I find a message from Veronica—

Hi Caitlin,

This is Veronica, writing from your dad's email, because I don't know how else to reach you.

I'm really sorry to tell you bad news like this in a letter, but your daddy is dead. He had a heart attack two days ago, and then another one this morning in the hospital, before they could get him into surgery. I know he was real upset about something and wanted to talk to you about it, but he didn't have your phone number and we couldn't find it on the Google.

Again, I'm sorry. I know you and Charles had your bad times, but he loved you, and was real proud.

He was sad he wasn't a better dad to all you kids, but proud of all of you, just the same.

I think we'll try to have the funeral sometime in the next couple days. Let me know if you and the kids are going to come. I'll just be getting the cheapest stuff they have unless I hear you want to chip in.

Real sorry,

Veronica

I freeze, my hand hovering over the mouse pad, my stomach sinking until it feels like it's going to fall straight through the floor. It looks like my wish from a moment ago came true—I'm never going to see my father again.

Heart in my throat, I close the laptop, cover my face with my hands, and cry as hard as I cried the day I lost the baby.

Gabe and Caitlin's story concludes in
A Love So Deep: Available Now

Keep reading for a sneak peek.

And subscribe to Lili's newsletter HERE **to make sure you never miss a sale or new release.**

SNEAK PEEK

Please enjoy this excerpt of
A LOVE SO DEEP
Available Now

Warning: Hold on tight for the red hot, adrenaline fueled conclusion to the To the Bone series.

What we have is sacred, a bond forged by pain and pleasure, suffering and passion, and Gabe is right—nothing will tear us apart again. This is forever, for keeps, for the rest of our lives, no matter what the future holds.

We just have to outsmart the powerful people determined to keep us apart.

I'm prepared to fight our enemies, but I'm not prepared for *him*. For a monster wearing a friendly face, or the nightmare he's determined to unleash.

They say it's better to have loved and lost than never to have loved at all. I say—over my dead body. They'll have to pry forever out of my cold, clawed hands.

A Love So Deep is the final book in the To the Bone series.

Excerpt

Gabe

"Tis in my memory lock'd,
And you yourself shall keep the key of it."
-Shakespeare

Before I was diagnosed with an allegedly inoperable brain tumor and nearly died, I had no interest in the obituary page.

I was young and immortal. I was going to live forever, go out in a blaze of glory, and I couldn't care less how many unlucky people had the misfortune to die on a given week.

After the surgery, I read the Giffney Gazette's

obituary page every Sunday morning, thumbing through the snapshots of lives lost as I linger over my coffee. It was only luck that kept me from gracing these pages. I feel obligated to read every entry, like I owe it to the people less fortunate than myself to read about the children and grandchildren they left behind, and the many adventures they had before they got old and set in their ways and hunkered down to waste the rest of their lives watching television.

But until today, I haven't known any of the recently deceased personally.

When I read that Charles Edwin Cooney has died at age fifty-four, leaving behind five children, and one grandchild, I can't say that I'm sad, but I feel the news. It hits me physically, tightening my throat, making my stomach clench around my second cup of coffee.

Chuck is dead, and one more avenue to finding Caitlin is closed forever.

Not like you've been looking too hard lately, anyway.

"What's wrong, dear?" My mother leans across the table, peering into my face, as attuned to my moods now as she has been since the moment I came out of surgery.

I don't remember my mother being this concerned about my emotional well-being last summer—or any of the twenty years before—but

Deborah is clearly trying to make the most of our second chance. She's determined to be the plugged-in parent she never was when I was growing up, no matter how irritating I find it, or how uncomfortable and strange this forced intimacy is for the both of us.

"I'm fine," I say, folding my paper in half. "Just read that Charles Cooney died."

I watch her face as she reacts, but her eyes are cool and unreadable, the way they always are when the Cooney name comes up in conversation. "Well, that's sad."

"It is," I say. "He was in his early fifties."

"That's what hard living will do to a person," my dad offers, not looking up from his own section of the paper, apparently unmoved by the news that my ex-girlfriend's father is dead.

According to my parents, they didn't know Caitlin and I were dating last summer. I kept our relationship a secret from them, and they have no clue what happened to her, or why we ended things. They're very convincing, but I know they're lying. I remember sitting next to Caitlin at this very table, running my hand up and down the silky soft skin of her thigh, thinking about all the things I wanted to do to her as soon as we were free of my parents.

But Deborah and Aaron don't know I'm recovering my memories.

Or that I *was* recovering them.

Since the night I saw Caitlin with the bruises on her throat, I've done my best to let sleeping demons lie. I keep my thoughts in the present, and steer clear of places that remind me of Caitlin. I take a sleeping pill before I go to bed, and I fuck Kimmy with a certain degree of reserve, not wanting to lose control and swing too close to the edge of the chasm. I don't want to glimpse the skeletons I sense are littering the ground on the other side. I'm afraid I'll learn something about myself that will make the surgery, and all the days I've fought to recover, pointless.

If I killed her, I don't deserve to be alive.

If I killed her, there is only one course of action I can take, and that would certainly be a waste, though I hear a good number of people like me do commit suicide. The post-operative fog, the feelings of alienation, and the sense that you will never be the person you were before—the person everyone in your life wants you to be so badly—is too much for a lot of people. They would rather check out, letting a bullet finish the job the tumor started.

"You won't go to the funeral will you?" Deborah asks, breaking into my thoughts.

I shake my head. "Why would I?"

Deborah looks flustered, but only for a

second. By the time she speaks, her cool has returned. "Of course not. Don't know what I was thinking." She smiles. "What about church? Are you joining us this morning? Might lift your spirits."

"My spirits are fine," I say, forcing a smile. "And I think I'd rather worship in my own way today. I'll probably take a ride, and meet you for lunch after."

My father chuckles. "I wish I could get away with worshiping in my own way."

"Your brand of worship involves way too much time on a fishing boat," my mother says, taking another sip of her coffee. "You're only home two days a week as it is. I'm not going to give up an entire day to the catfish in Lake Anderson."

"You could go with him," I suggest, though it's hard to imagine my perfectly pulled together mother baking in the sun on a fishing boat.

Deborah raises one thin, blond brow. The dubious expression on her face makes me smile. Sometimes I like Deborah, even if she is a manipulative liar. Considering my own, checkered history, I'm not really in any position to judge.

"Sorry, must have been the tumor hole talking." I stand and circle the table, leaning down to kiss her cheek. "See you at noon."

"We're going to Peabody's on the square,"

Deborah says, patting my arm. "The Jamisons are coming, and I've only got reservations for six, so don't bring a guest."

I clench my jaw, biting back the smartass remark on the tip of my tongue. I know which "guest" Deborah is talking about, but there's no point in getting into an argument about Kimmy. If Kimmy and I hadn't run into my mother at the grocery store last week, Deborah never would have met my latest fling.

Kimmy and I are fuck buddies, nothing more. I don't plan on keeping in touch after I leave for school, and Kimmy doesn't even know how long she'll be in town. She has a six-month lease, and a job as a cocktail waitress, but no real ties to Giffney. This is just the place she ended up when her money for bus fare ran out. She has dreams of moving home to Louisiana and opening a fabric store, and I have dreams of going back to the university, picking up where I left off, and pretending this long, strange detour never happened.

Or at least that's one of the lies I tell myself.

What I really want is something very different.

What I want is for this hole inside of me to be filled up with something. Someone. I want to know Caitlin wasn't a dream, and that I'm not a monster.

And so, when I hear my parents' car pull down the driveway on their way to church, I don't go to the barn to saddle my horse. I head down to the Beamer and drive into town, across the railroad tracks, to the ranch house where Caitlin used to live.

A Love So Deep
is Available Now

TELL LILI YOUR FAVORITE PART!

I love reading your thoughts about the books and your review matters. Reviews help readers find new-to-them authors to enjoy. So if you could take a moment to leave a review letting me know your favorite part of the story—nothing fancy required, even a sentence or two would be wonderful—I would be deeply grateful.

ABOUT THE AUTHOR

Author of over forty novels, *USA Today* Bestseller **Lili Valente** writes everything from steamy suspense to laugh-out-loud romantic comedies. A die-hard romantic, she can't resist a story where love wins big. Because love should always win. She lives in Vermont with her two big-hearted boy children and a dog named Pippa Jane.

Find Lili at...
www.lilivalente.com

Find Lili at www.lilivalente.com

Seduced

Sparked

Scooped

Hot Royal Romance

The Playboy Prince

The Grumpy Prince

The Bossy Prince

Laugh-out-Loud Rocker Rom Coms

The Bangover

Bang Theory

Banging The Enemy

The Rock Star's Baby Bargain

The Bliss River Small Town Series

Falling for the Fling

Falling for the Ex

Falling for the Bad Boy

The Hunter Brothers

The Baby Maker

The Troublemaker

The Heartbreaker

The Panty Melter

Bad Motherpuckers Series

Hot as Puck

Sexy Motherpucker

Puck-Aholic

Puck me Baby

Pucked Up Love

Puck Buddies

The Lonesome Point Series

(Sexy Cowboys)

Leather and Lace

Saddles and Sin

Diamonds and Dust

12 Dates of Christmas

Glitter and Grit

Sunny with a Chance of True Love

Chaps and Chance

Ropes and Revenge

8 Second Angel

The Good Love Series

(co-written with Lauren Blakely)

The V Card

Good with His Hands

Good to be Bad